Leo Kessler is a familiar name to readers of war fiction. In addition to his numerous super-selling war series he is the author of several non-fiction works and of the screenplay *Breakthr* … Germany between energetic bouts of t …

Also by Leo Kessler

The *SS Assault Regiment Wotan* Series
SS PANZER BATTALION
DEATH'S HEAD
CLAWS OF STEEL
GUNS AT CASSINO
THE DEVIL'S SHIELD
HAMMER OF THE GODS
FORCED MARCH
BLOOD AND ICE
THE SAND PANTHERS
COUNTER-ATTACK
PANZER HUNT
SLAUGHTER GROUND
HELLFIRE
FLASHPOINT
CAULDRON OF BLOOD
SCHIRMER'S HEADHUNTERS
WHORES OF WAR
SCHIRMER'S DEATH LEGION

The *Stormtroop* Series
STORMTROOP
BLOOD MOUNTAIN
VALLEY OF THE ASSASSINS
RED ASSAULT
HIMMLER'S GOLD
FIRE OVER KABUL
WAVE OF TERROR

The *Otto Stahl* Series
OTTO'S PHONEY WAR
OTTO'S BLITZKRIEG!
OTTO AND THE REDS

The *Sea Wolves* Series
SINK THE SCHARNHORST!
DEATH TO THE DEUTSCHLAND

Also:
As Klaus Konrad
The *Russian* Series
FIRST BLOOD
MARCH ON MOSCOW
FRONT SWINE

Leo Kessler

Otto Stahl 4
Otto and the Yanks

Futura
Macdonald & Co
London & Sydney

A Futura Book

First published in Great Britain in 1983
by Futura Publications, a Division of
Macdonald & Co (Publishers) Ltd
London & Sydney

ISBN 0 7088 2313 0

Filmset, printed and bound in Great Britain by
Hazell Watson & Viney Ltd, Aylesbury, Bucks

Futura Publications
A Division of
Macdonald & Co (Publishers) Ltd
Maxwell House
74 Worship Street
London EC2A 2EN

AUTHOR'S NOTE

The question I asked myself when I first read Herr Stahl's amazing revelations about that year of 1943 was, 'Could the Allied conquest of Sicily and the subsequent events in mainland Italy really have happened this way?' Was the Allies' first venture back into Europe, after the debacle of Dunkirk three years before, simply a great game played between US General Patton and his British rival Bernard Law Montgomery with personal glory and the kudos of victory as the stakes and the Germans merely extras in an extravaganza?

These were the sort of urgent questions I posed to Herr Stahl in his Spanish hideout after I had read the first draft of this, the fourth volume of his personal history of World War Two. As usual he reacted angrily, waving his cane at me and nearly knocking over the glass of *Pernod*, which he now drinks habitually *before* breakfast. (His explanation for this idiosyncratic behaviour: 'I've got to get the shitting creative juices working somehow every morning.')

'What in three devils' name do you know about it, Kessler?' came his explosive reply to my questions. 'You *weren't* there. I *was*! Take my word for it. That's the way things were in Sicily in 1943. And I'll tell you this for free, Kessler, all generals, whether they're white, black or green, limey, kraut, russki or wop, are out for the same thing. However many dead stubble-hoppers it takes to do it, they're out for *GLORY*! And yer Yank generals are the worst of the lot,' he had added with a sneer on his wrinkled old face, 'they don't only want glory, *they want sex as well!*'

I suppose he was right about the generals. They always

have been a strange bunch, and the reality behind most battles and wars does indeed differ greatly from those idealistic patriotic accounts presented in the average school history book. It is not commonly known for instance that Napoleon spent most of the Battle of Waterloo squatting behind sundry bushes and boulders suffering from acute diarrhoea; nor that Lord Cardigan rode out of the 'jaws of Death' after the Charge of the Light Brigade, ticked off one of the few survivors for having his shako on at a wrong angle, went back to his yacht (yes, his Lordship actually fought the war from his private yacht), had a bath, a champagne dinner and then dismissing the servants rogered his mistress in the salon; nor indeed that 'the Hero of Verdun', Marshal Petain, was summoned from a Parisian brothel to take command of that immortal defence – not bad going for a man who was already sixty-nine; and that Petain's great opponent the German General Ludendorff spent much of 1918 hoping that the French would break with the English so that French battleships could sail up the Thames and blast the capital to smithereens. Yes, a very strange bunch of individuals indeed.

But could they really have been as strange as Otto Stahl has portrayed them in these scurrilous *memoirs* of his? I don't know. All I know is that working with Herr Stahl always reminds me of a cartoon I once saw in the *New Yorker*. It depicted a man falling off the top of the Empire State Building. On the way down some smart-assed New Yorker leans out of a window on the twentieth floor and shouts, 'How's it going, fella?' to which the suicide replies, with a grin, 'All right, *so far!*'

Let us, therefore, not push Herr Stahl's credibility to its final end. I'll leave you, gentle reader, to make your own decisions about it. It's all right – *so far* . . .'

Leo Kessler,
Hamburg, W. Germany, 1981

VOLUME FOUR OF THE WARTIME MEMORIES OF OTTO STAHL JULY–SEPT 1943

'Call up the Army and the Navy!
Call up the rank and file!
Call up the gallant territorials –
They'll save England with a smile!
Call up the boys and the old diehards
To fight so England can be free!
Call up my brother,
My sister or my mother.
BUT FOR GAWDSAKE, DON'T TAKE ME!'

Herr O. Stahl's most favourite song.

'It takes 16,000 dead to train the average major general.'

Marshal Joffre, 1916

PART ONE: OLE BLOOD AN' GUTS

'War is a killing business. You've got to spill their blood or they'll spill yours. Rip 'em up the belly, or shoot 'em in the guts.' *Favourite speech of General 'Blood an' Guts' Patton to new recruits.*

ONE

'Willya just get a load of the cocky little bastard!' General Patton moaned through gritted teeth and stared down at the sunlit courtyard below. He shifted his big cigar from one side of his thin, cruel mouth to the other and snarled. 'Now he's gonna go into his usual act. The bastard should have been on Broadway.'

Down below, the small, ferret-faced English General with his beak of a nose had mounted the bonnet of the jeep standing in the middle of a rigid square of immaculately clad soldiers.

Otto Stahl and his friend the Count, along with the rest of Patton's staff, strained to get a good view of Montgomery. He was just beginning the set speech he had been making throughout the coastal regions ever since fighting in North Africa had ceased the month before.

'Now the little limey sonuvabitch is gonna make it in my own backyard,' Patton growled beneath his breath.

'I've come up here this afternoon, chaps,' came Montgomery's high-pitched, dispassionate voice, 'to tell you a bit about the party we'll soon be having on the other side of the water.' With a gesture he indicated the clean blue sweep of the Mediterranean sparkling in the afternoon sun. 'It's going to be a ripping good party, too. That I can tell you. Really going to hit them for six this time, what!'

He beamed at his wooden-faced audience of British officers squinting against the sun. Above, Patton clapped his hand to his forehead in mock despair. 'Christ in Heaven,' he cried, 'now he's on to that damned cricket of his!'

Otto's keen blue eyes flashed from the English officers and back to the Americans clustered around their commander: they were all like actors in an amateur theatre group, always nodding knowingly, always ready to laugh at any joke made by their general, eager for any trivial piece of gossip. 'You know what, Count,' he whispered out of the side of his mouth to his white-haired companion, 'since I've got to know these Amis, I've come to this conclusion.'

'What Otto, my boy?'

'The Amis are not fighting Hitler really. They're fighting the Tommies. That's what this war in the Med is really about.'

The good-looking Count who had taken to chewing gum and speaking German in an 'American' accent ever since they had been recruited to General Patton's cause a few weeks ago, whispered, 'Well, the English think they've got a monopoly on this war because they got into it first. It's about time our American boys had a chance.'

Otto groaned at 'our American boys'. It was typical of the Count's fatal weakness for self-dramatization. Once again he had forgotten he was a German; he was now a full-blooded fighting American. Otto lapsed into silence and tried to catch up on the speech being made below.

'We've bowled Rommel a googly here in Africa. Now we're going to do the same sort of job on the other side. But how, what?' Montgomery winked craftily and a young subaltern in the rear rank, who had over-indulged in the mess that lunch and could no longer contain himself, let go a juicy fart. 'No coughing please, gentlemen,' Montgomery said, 'until I give you permission! Now old Winnie said to me the other day, "Monty, you really must get cracking." I said to Winnie – very great man by the way, "Not on, sir. Can't knock 'em for six until we've got all our bits and pieces right, what?" ' He glared suddenly at his sweating audience, whose uniforms were turning black with perspiration in the afternoon heat.

' "Mustn't play on a sticky wicket," I said, "can't have that, PM." "Why not?" says he. I say, "Never put my chaps on to bat unless I'm sure they're going to knock up a century. If they're going to do the job right, PM, they'll need two hundred more Shermans, another brigade of paratroops, four hundred more twenty-five pounders . . .".' The little General reeled off the list of deadly weapons in a dry matter-of-fact tone, as if he were checking a domestic grocer's list.

Patton gave another deep groan and said, 'Gentlemen, let us get back to our planning before he starts demanding support of Almighty God himself!' He turned, gritting his dingy sawn-off teeth, as below Montgomery droned on about 'hitting the Boche for six in Sicily' and 'keeping after him like a terrier after a rat'.

Otto and the Count followed the high-ranking staff into the pleasant coolness of a large room hung with situation maps and provided with a gently rotating fan which cooled the air and made the maps flap, as if they were alive and impatient to be released.

Patton sat down in his big leather armchair, crossed his elegantly booted legs, rested his twin ivory-handled forty-fives more comfortably and nodded to his Chief of Intelligence, Colonel Carl Dickson, 'All right, Monk, shoot the works,' he commanded and putting on his War Face Number Four, a ferocious look which he practised assiduously before the bedroom mirror when he was alone, glared in the direction of that rasping upper-class English voice.

The tall, bespectacled Intelligence Chief took up his stance in the centre of the room and indicated, with his pointer, the map of the Mediterranean which dominated the place. 'Sicily, our next objective as you all know, gentlemen. According to the latest information at our disposal, it is defended by six static Eyetie divisions along the coast, with four field divisions further inland, backed up by two Kraut divisions, including the Hermann Goering Panzer, both, gentlemen,' Dickson looked hard at his listeners, as if he wished to impress the fact upon them, 'strictly hot mustard!'

Otto looked down gloomily at his American Army issue shoes. For nearly four years now he had been trying to avoid combat in a war which he would not fight for Adolf Hitler; all the same, the mention of German troops always made him feel uneasy – and somehow a traitor.

The Count, for his part, seemed to have no such inhibitions. He was eagerly soaking in the information being imparted by the tall Intelligence officer, his large eyes, which Otto thought resembled peeled, hard-boiled eggs, full of excitement.

'Now when the going gets tough,' Dickson said, 'the Boche will pull the plug on the Eyeties and wash them down the drain. All the same those Eyetie field divisions could hold up our advance in Central Sicily on account of the rugged terrain. So Intelligence considers our advance – once we get off the beach in Sicily – will be slow.'

'*Slow!*' Patton barked. 'Yeah, that's the goddam catch. So we barrel through the Eyeties on the beach and then we start having to slog it out with those inland, while Bernard Law Montgomery grabs all the glory of capturing Syracuse, Catania and Messina. He'll make the headlines while I have to make do with the boondocks. My publicity will be shot to all hell.'

'Don't you worry, General,' Roaring Red Rory's hearty voice broke into the heavy mournful silence which had greeted General Patton's outburst. 'We're gonna have *names, names, names*, come hell or high water!' He pushed back his helmet which bore the boldly stencilled white letters 'AAA-O', meaning 'Anything, anytime, anywhere – bar nothing', the motto of Patton's personal publicity department. 'We've got a plan.'

'*A plan?*' the assembled staff officers echoed as one.

'*A plan!*' Roaring Red said triumphantly, looking pointedly at the Count.

Otto's heart sank when he saw that look. He knew it meant one thing for Mrs Stahl's handsome son – *trouble!*

Outside General Montgomery was saying confidently, 'we'll pick out a couple of hundred yards of beach, pound it with the Navy, bash it with the Air Force, fling in our chaps and knock the wops for six . . .'

'What kind of plan?' Patton asked slowly, his War Face Number Four giving way to Imperious Roman Emperor Number Two. 'What kind of malarky have you dreamed up now, Red?'

Roaring Red gave his chief a sly grin. 'General, how would you like to get to Messina first instead of that limey?'

'I would like it very much,' Patton answered, still holding his imperial look. 'Very much indeed.' He waved a beringed hand at the big grinning ex-film executive, whose job it was to ensure that he obtained the maximum amount of publicity from any of his wartime exploits. 'Give?'

'Well, General, old Monk here has just mentioned that the Krauts have two divisions on the island, including this here Hermann Goering Panzer, commanded by Baron von Bork—'

'*Borkenheim*,' hastily the Count supplied the correct name and Otto's heart sank even further. A dark inkling started to grow in the back of his mind.

'Thank you, Count. Well, sir, what if we could manage to sic this Kraut's division on to Montgomery just after he's hit the beaches?'

'*Sic him on to Montgomery!*' If the big General had at that moment ripped open his breeches and waved his wand at them, his staff officers' excited reaction would have been no different, Otto thought cynically.

Patton's eyes narrowed. Slowly, very slowly, he rose to his feet. He crossed to where his lacquered helmet with its three outsize gold stars on the front rested and placed it carefully on his balding head. 'Gentlemen, I shall now go and take tea with the limeys. I have not heard one word of your disreputable plot, for George S. Patton Junior would be ashamed to be associated with such an underhand scheme, whatever form it may take.' Suddenly he shot the crestfallen officer one of his dingy, stub-toothed smiles. 'But there's sure as hell going to be some heads rolling in this staff if I don't get to Messina before Bernard Law Montgomery! Good afternoon to you.'

As the planners clicked to attention, General Patton swaggered out, leaving his fat-bellied officers to stare at his ramrod-straight khaki back with admiration and undisguised adulation.

TWO

With due ceremony the two Generals acknowledged the salute of the two MPs guarding the general officers' latrine and then scurried past the sign reading '*Reserved strictly for one star generals – by Order of the Provost Marshal.*'

Standing side by side in the urinals the tall American and the under-sized Englishman made a great play of fumbling impressively inside their flies, as if intent on dragging out some enormous snake. Finally, ego satisfied, both sighed with relief as the urine started to stream out.

'Tea!' Montgomery explained.

'Bourbon!' Patton answered, absorbed in his task.

The drunken singing of officers whom Montgomery had addressed that afternoon filtered through to the pissing generals, '*There's a shortage of good bints in Matruh, There's a shortage of good bints in Matruh. So you pull it till you wince. Then you tie it up in splints. In Matruh, in Matruh, in Matruh . . .*'

Montgomery frowned with distaste and Patton said with a grin, 'Yours, I think.'

Montgomery's response was quicker than Patton had expected. 'How's your beach, Georgie?' he asked with what he took to be a winning smile.

'Bloody, Monty!' he snapped, grin gone now. 'More exposed than yours and with open sand bars – *and* I've only got one small port for my supplies.'

Montgomery watered the white tile expertly and said, 'They're only wops you know, Georgie. No trouble there. Besides what do you need a big port for? You won't need much in the way of supplies for stooging around in Central

Sicily, what.' He finished and began to fasten the stiff brass buttons of his battledress flies.

Perhaps it was the bourbon or perhaps it was Patton's natural hot temper, the American General didn't know what made him make the wager, all he knew afterwards was that he wished he hadn't, but that was later. 'Stooging around!' he exploded. 'My Seventh Army doesn't stooge around, Monty!' He assumed his Number One Misunderstood Genius First Class Look and looked down his long nose at the little Englishman. 'I'm not a betting man, Monty, but I wager you five English pounds here and now that my Seventh will be in Messina twenty-four hours before your Eighth.'

'Did you say Messina, Georgie?' Montgomery paused in what he was doing and looked curiously at his big companion.

'Yes I did – for five quid. Are you on, Monty?'

'You'll be losing a fiver, you know?'

'On or not?' Patton snapped.

'Why of course. Let me wash my hands and I'll shake on it.' Montgomery crossed to the wash-basin at the far end of the urinal. In the flyblown mirror he caught a glimpse of Patton's face as he fastened his breeches. 'Good grief,' he said to himself, 'the chap really is dead confident he's going to pull it off. *Why?*'

Five minutes later they had agreed their wager and General Bernard Law Montgomery was making an urgent phone call to a tiny office in a remote part of his HQ with the innocuous designation on its peeling door, 'Office of Civilian Sub-Contracting'.

Outside the drunken young officers sang, '*The kitehawks, they fly high in Matruh. The kitehawks they fly high. Then they swoop down from the sky. And they shit right in your eye. In Matruh, in Matruh, in Matruh . . .*'

'I have known Benno von Borkenheim for years now, since

1916 to be exact,' the Count was saying at the very moment that Montgomery was making his mysterious telephone call. 'He's a real fire-raiser and what might be called a collector, or *connoisseur*, of multiple wounds.' He beamed at the big red-headed American Colonel, obviously pleased at the way he had phrased it.

Behind them in the big room, the planning staff had broken up into syndicates once more, each group responsible for some aspect or other of the great invasion. A plaintive Mid-Western voice was saying, 'But I insist that the rubbers go in in the second wave. What say the boys land and find there's one of them mobile Eyetie cathouses on the beach? They'd be defenceless without their rubbers.'

'What do you mean, Count, "connoisseur of wounds"?' Roaring Red Rory Mulligan asked and scratched his flies as if the mention of rubbers had had some effect upon him.

'He was always getting pieces of himself shot or chopped off, Colonel, that's why. His right eye's gone and left arm. Kneecap made of stainless steel. What else? Oh yes, he's got a silver plate in the back of his head.'

'What's his dong made of,' Otto asked sourly, mind still reeling at the thought of Red Rory's bold, impossible plan to ensure that Patton captured Messina first, '*plastic?*'

But the two other men ignored him. Red Rory was saying, 'This Baron friend of yours is kinda careless, isn't he, Count?'

'Not really, Colonel. It's just he always likes to march to the sound of the guns. I remember back in '17, when I was a young cavalry officer, he'd just had an eye shot out in the trenches and been told in Berlin that he couldn't go back to France with one eye. So he bought himself a perfectly impossible glass eye, stuck it into the empty socket and convinced the board to let him go back to fight. Once outside, I remember seeing him hail a cab to take him to the nearest station to catch the next troop train for the front and hurling his glass eye out of the window as it drove off. What a chap!'

There was a moment's silence and over at the syndicates, the Mid-Westerner was protesting, 'But if you send baseballs in in the third wave, Sam, surely rubbers should go in in the second! Hot shit, for ya average red-blooded American boy, sex comes before sport any day!'

'So you think this Baron guy will take the bait, Count?'

'Oh very definitely,' the Count answered, as always carried away with enthusiasm at the prospect of a new adventure. 'With all due respect, your General Patton is a very good general, but he is an unknown quantity to the *Wehrmacht*. There'll be a few kudos in beating him.'

Red Rory frowned at 'beating', but said nothing and the Count continued, his plump face flushed with excitement.

'Montgomery is a different story. If Benno von Borkenheim can beat him, especially after the drubbing he gave Rommel recently here in Africa, it will very definitely be a feather in his cap. He'll jump at the chance.'

Red Rory rubbed the side of his craggy scarlet face, the face of a man who over-indulged in expensive cigars and bottles of bourbon. 'You know, Count, from the way you tell it I think we can say the project's off the ground. It sounds to me like a very viable programme. What say we give it a whirl. What've we got to lose, eh?'

Otto Stahl's handsome young face flushed angrily. 'What've we got to lose!' he exclaimed. 'Oh not much, just our damned heads?' He glared at the Count and snapped in German, 'What's wrong with you, you old fart? Don't you realize that if we're caught over there by our own people, we're straight for the Gestapo and the short sharp kiss-off! And if the Tommies catch us, they'll have the turnips off us in the Tower of London for treachery – *with an axe!*'

Red Rory looked back and forth in bewilderment and cried, 'Woah, there, boys! Enough of that kraut talk. What gives?'

Otto, his blue eyes now blazing with anger, stared back. 'I'll tell you what gives, Colonel! Ever since 1939 I've been trying to keep myself out of the firing line and save my precious head. Why? – because I'm a devout coward. But what happens? I'll tell you. Ever since I met this old cunt here,' he indicated the Count with an angry wave of his hand, 'I've been landed in the shit time and time again. I nearly have my balls sawn off in Holland[1] by a crazy Dutch cavalryman. I get captured by the English[2] and sent on a crazy mission to rescue Churchill's homo bastard. I'm raped by a sex-mad female commissar in Russia,[3] and because Dago pilot couldn't find his way into a whore's bed, we land up here. Just when I've told myself I've opted out of this war for good, this old c—'

'Count, *please*, Otto,' the Count pleaded. 'Not that vile word!'

Otto swallowed hard, controlling himself with the greatest of difficulty, 'gets us into another impossible mission.'

Red Rory beamed down at him. 'But don't you see, that's why the American Army needs you. You're the experts, the professionals. You know the ropes, the tricks of the trade. The American Army couldn't hope of fielding a couple of professionals like you. Besides the Count here has told me how you've always been in the German resistance right from the start. By carrying out this mission you're helping to speed up Hitler's downfall.'

'Helping to put General Patton in the headlines more likely,' Otto growled.

Red Rory did not seem to hear. 'One day Germany will honour you both for the great patriots you are.'

'That is if the Gestapo don't shorten us by a head first.' Otto folded his arms stubbornly across his chest and declared firmly, 'The Count can do what he damn well likes! But I'm not going. And that's final.'

The Count looked at his companion aghast. 'Otto, you can't be serious?' he exclaimed.

'I've never been more serious in my life!' Otto snapped,

[1] See *OTTO'S PHONEY WAR*
[2] see *OTTO'S BLITZKRIEG!*
[3] see *OTTO AND THE REDS*.

and then in German, 'I've had a noseful of you and your shitting amateur dramatics. I am not going!'

'Otto you—' the Count began, but Red Rory cut him short with an upraised hand.

'Just one moment, Count,' he said. Then turning to the enraged Otto, the usual good-humoured twinkle now gone from his blood-shot eyes, said gravely, 'Otto, I hate to do this to you kid, but I'm gonna lay one on you.'

'What do you mean?'

Behind them the syndicates had finally solved the problem of the Mid-Westerner's contraceptives – they would go in in the second wave. They'd follow the assault infantry of the Big Red One[1] and land together with the Coca-Cola and the Hershey Bars. 'One guy in the line and five guys to bring up the Coca-Cola,' the officer who had objected said cynically, but apparently no one was listening any longer.

Red Rory had taken his time to answer, but finally he turned to Otto and said, 'Look at it this way, Otto. My first duty is to General Patton, however much I might like you and the Count. I'm his publicity manager, as you might say, and he's got to score in Sicily if he wants to get into the big league. So friend, I'm gonna have to come the heavy with you to ensure that he does score.'

Suddenly Otto had that well-known uneasy feeling that the military machine had grabbed him again in its steel clutches and there was no escaping it. It had been the same in Germany, then in England and finally in Russia. Fear and apprehension traced a slow cold finger down his spine.

'Last week we came to an agreement with the Swiss Red Cross to repatriate a bunch of severely wounded Krauts from Algiers back to the Fatherland. They'll never fight again so they're no danger. The Limeys have done the same thing before and got some of their own guys back in return. We're hoping Berlin will let us have some of our boys in exchange who were caught in that snafu at the

[1] Nickname for the 1st US Infantry Division

Kasserine Pass in the spring. No matter.' He paused momentarily, as if he was considering his words well before he said them. 'Now what say we included you in that transport, Otto? And what say we passed the word to them wounded Krauts that you weren't altogether what you were supposed to be? And what say the Gestapo found a thousand dollars in your hold gear once you got back to the Fatherland? And what say—'

Numbly Otto held out his hands, as if for handcuffing, head bent in defeat. 'All right, Colonel, you've convinced me you can force me. There's nothing I can do but go.'

Colonel Mulligan's craggy face broke into a huge smile and he slapped Otto heartily on the back. 'I knew you'd see it my way, Otto. Attaboy! All right, fellers, this is the deal. You report tomorrow for your briefing at zero eight hundred hours sharp. Okay?'

'And where exactly do we report, sir?' asked the Count, his face now wreathed in smiles.

'The Kasbah. The goldsmith's near the northern entrance to the place.'

'The Kasbah!' The Count drew in his breath sharply like a Japanese peasant might meeting the Mikado in his paddy-field. 'Oh, I say, how impossibly romantic! The Kasbah! It takes me back to the good old days with the *Abwehr*[1] before this war came along and lowered the whole standard of espionage.' His dark eyes took on a melodramatic look of passionate secret longing, tinged with mystery and intrigue. 'I think I'm going to like this one,' he declared.

'I'm sure you are, Count,' Red Rory boomed in hearty agreement. 'And remember you're doing it for the freedom-loving West and the future of democracy.'

Otto Stahl clapped his hand to his head in mock wonder. 'Freedom-loving West and the future of democracy!' he groaned. *'Great Crap on the Christmas Tree – here we go again . . .'*

[1] The German Secret Service

THREE

It was still early, yet already the steep narrow streets leading up from the sea to Algiers' famed Kasbah were packed with loud, smelly, jostling crowds. Little sleepy-eyed boys stood in dark doorways eating bowls of cold white beans as they chanted their wares. Plump women swathed from head to toe in black swayed by, balancing their purchases on their heads. Purveyors of coffee hawked their beverage among the throng, their little glass cups jingling at their waists. Fishermen, barefoot and scaly-legged, pushed barrows full of dried octopi to the waiting stalls; and from behind the closed shutters – for already the sun was hot – there came the long dying wail of an Arab singer.

'How typical, Otto,' the Count, his fat trusting face already gleaming with sweat, breathed enthusiastically. 'How very typical – and the colour of it all!'

Otto wiped the sweat off his forehead and aimed a half-hearted kick at a skinny-ribbed dog which had dared to raise its leg against his boot. 'It pongs,' he said sourly. 'As if they'd opened up all the shitlines back in Berlin-Kreuzberg.'

The Count sighed and continued up the steep alley. 'You have no soul, Otto.'

A large woman, her massive bosom draped in a Union Jack, leaned over a balcony, bearing what looked like a bottle of whisky in her hamlike fist. 'You like jig-jig, soldiers?' she asked in heavily accented English. *Blow it, throw it, row it! I give you something new.*' The effort of all that talking made her bosom and jowls tremble like jelly and the Count dodged back hastily, as if he half-expected one of her mighty breasts to fall off and engulf him.

'Yer, like leprosy, perhaps,' Otto sneered.

The whore held up her fat middle finger. 'You sit on that, nancy boy!' she cried in disgust and parting the beadwork on the balcony, she swished indignantly from sight.

'Ah, the romance of the Kasbah!' Otto said cynically and, stepping through the northern entrance into the ancient rambling market, felt suddenly oppressed by its gloomy darkness after the bright sunshine outside.

For a moment the Count and Otto stood there indecisively, bewildered by the mass of open-fronted shops, with everywhere robed men squatting on their haunches busily hammering away at metal, leather, wood, as if they expected a whole fleet of tourists to descend upon them at any moment and clamour for their wares.

Then Otto spotted the goldsmith's place. 'Over there,' he said, 'next to that one with the dried camel-pizzle hanging from the front.'

'My God,' the Count shuddered as they passed the great black leathery-looking camel penis hanging from the frame of the leather-shop, 'the poor animal *must* have been sick!'

Otto looked up at the thing, which must have been all of sixty centimetres in length and said drily, 'I should be *that* sick!' Together they entered the goldsmith's.

Squatted on a metal-littered bench opposite the door a small man with a great beak of a nose dominating his swarthy face hammered away at a piece of gold wire held between his skinny knees. In the far corner a man who appeared to be either a monk or a friar stood with his back to the newcomers, peering at the goods displayed there. The air was heavy with the odour of charcoal, garlic and unusual smelling tobacco.

The Count cleared his throat. '*Bonjour*,' he said hesitantly. The little goldsmith in the dirty *burnous* looked up and said, '*Bonjour, Guten Morgen, Buenos Dias, salaam,* good morning,' reeling off the greeting like a litany, while beaming at them as if his very life depended upon it. 'You wish?'

The question confused the Count. Suddenly he realized he didn't know who was to receive them here to brief them on the first stage of their mission to Sicily. 'I'd thought –' he began in English when the monk or friar wandered over and said quietly in an unmistakable American accent, 'Hi, guys. Just mozzy on in, pretending you're looking at this junk. I'll follow. You just can't be too careful on a mission like this, there are gooks spying for the Krauts everywhere in the Kasbah.'

To his surprise Otto saw the religious man had a fat cigar clamped in the corner of his mouth and a love-bite obviously made by some over-amorous woman on the side of his cheek. Once again, his heart sank; he was back with the spy nuts.

A few moments later the strange monk had joined them in the dark smelly corridor to the rear of the little goldsmith, who worked on, eyes fixed cautiously on the door.

'Count von der Weide and Herr Otto Stahl?' he asked and stretched out a big hand, his broad, good-humoured face wreathed in smiles. 'Been expecting you. Welcome aboard. Lieutenant Al Cheetham, Algiers Section OSS[1], code-named "Friar Tuck".' He indicated his garb with his free hand. 'I'm attached to the local chapter of the Mission to Seamen. Wouldn't turn my back on a single one of 'em in this skirt!'

The American seized first the Count's hand and then Otto's and shook them as if he were practising squeezing apples to pulp in one go.

'We've heard a lot about you guys. You're the real professionals, I hear.'

'Thank you – er – Friar Tuck,' the Count said, beaming all over his face; and then to Otto. 'My boy, it's just like

[1] Forerunner of the CIA

the old days with the *Abwehr* back in '39, isn't it? Costumes and code-names and everything.'

Otto said nothing; he couldn't.

'Come on, guys,' Friar Tuck said, chomping his cigar from one side of his mouth to the other, 'let's go and meet the CO . . .' He hesitated just a fraction of a second, 'I'd like to warn you that he's got some . . . er . . . rather strange habits. Okay, let's go.'

'*Wipem's the name!*' a tall thin man dressed completely in black barked from behind his desk, as the two friends and their guide entered the dark backroom, 'Hardiman Wipem, code-named – "*the Beast*"! As if to emphasize the point, he brought his thin black riding crop down hard on the table making its contents rattle and the Count jump. Behind him leaning against the wall, a skinny, yellow-faced sailor smoked a cigarette, eyes wrinkled to slits, the quarter he constantly spun moving up and down in a gleam of silver.

'Glad to meet you,' the Count said and held out his hand apprehensively, as if he expected the American with the thin cruel mouth and daunting eyebrows which met above his thin chiselled nose to strike it with his switch.

Wipem ignored the hand. 'I demand instant obedience!' he snarled and brought the switch down once more. 'I will not tolerate the slightest hesitation. I have orders to ensure that you are landed in Sicily and then conveyed to the headquarters of Baron von Borkenheim, Commander of the Hermann Goering Panzer Division.' Again he slammed down the switch. 'I shall carry out those orders.' A fat blue fly buzzed into the room. It was a foolish thing to do.

Captain Wipem's dark eyes gleamed with sudden animation. His free hand flashed out. With a grunt of pleasure he squashed the fly and let it drop on to the desk, the surface of which was already littered with similarly crushed insects. '*Kill them, kill all of them!*' Wipem hissed, a thin trail of saliva emerging from the side of his mouth. 'They bring disease and dirt! They have to be wiped out – *mercilessly*!'

Otto was suddenly overcome by the unreasoning conviction that if this strange American opened his mouth wide, he would see a neat row of needle-sharp teeth, a vampire's teeth.

'Now where was I?' Wipem asked, his voice suddenly normal.

'They have to be wiped out mercilessly,' Friar Tuck said and Otto thought he could hear a chuckle in the Lieutenant's voice.

'No, I didn't mean that,' Wipem snorted and brought his switch down once more. 'Oh yes, now then you two, you might be regarded in some quarters as professionals, but to my eye you look fat, flabby and flat-footed. Not at all fit for the task ahead of you.' Without looking round, he cried, 'Carlo, the knife!'

The man leaning against the wall dropped his quarter and with startling speed his hand flashed to his pocket and a wicked-looking knife quivered threateningly at the feet of a suddenly white-faced, trembling Count.

'See what I mean?' Wipem barked. 'Reactions slow. If Carlo had so wished, you would be dead now.'

Otto clenched his fist deliberately. 'Listen,' he said slowly, 'tell that spaghetti-eater of yours,' he indicated Carlo who was flipping another quarter up and down as if nothing had happened, 'that if he pulls another damn fool trick like that, I'll carve the ears off him with his own carving-knife. Clear?'

'It was just a little joke, Herr Stahl,' Friar Tuck intervened hastily. 'The CO likes to have his little jokes, don't you – er – Beast?'

Wipem looked at his subordinate coldly. 'I have never joked or laughed in my whole life, Friar Tuck,' he said.

'That I can well believe,' Otto said grimly under his breath.

'Now we have ten days before your mission goes in,' he

said. 'Till then I'm taking you out to Djebel Djurjura for a five-day hardening-up course under my personal supervision.' Again he slapped down his cane. 'The remaining five will be devoted to your jumps.'

'Jumps?' the Count asked innocently.

'Yes,' Wipem answered severely. 'I have not the slightest hope of making you into anything approximating a trained para, but at least I can teach you the rudiments in that time.'

'Rudiments of what – er – Beast?' the Count persisted.

'My God, man, you really are slow! Didn't they tell you at HQ? *You are going to be parachuted into Sicily.*'

FOUR

'Back at Fort Bragg,' the Beast snapped, squinting into the bright white sun, 'they take five months to train a paratrooper. I'm going to train you guys in exactly five days.'

The Count and Otto standing at the edge of the bone-dry desert gorge looked at him stonily. He was still dressed in black, complete with leather gloves in spite of the burning heat, and as always he emphasized his words with slaps of his leather switch against his leg. It seemed he could not refrain from his own peculiar kind of physical punctuation.

'Of course, there'll be a few cuts and bruises. But what do they matter?' His dark cruel eyes gleamed with the same animation Otto had observed when he had crushed the fly six days before. 'Some people are said to like that sort of thing.'

'Yer,' Otto said sourly under his breath, eyeing the taut steel wire stretched across the gorge by two high wooden posts, 'I know who.'

By this time he thought he knew what made the Beast tick. In the five previous days of 'hardening up' which they had spent in Djebel Djurjura the American had disappeared into his tent among the palms each night with one of the willing dark-eyed Arab boys who inhabited the oasis; and the warm night had been full of the rhythmic thwack-thwack of his cane and the shrieks, feigned or genuine, of the paid youth. A grinning Friar Tuck had commented one night while the three of them squatted around a flickering fire, 'Well as the limeys would say, the CO's having a *smashing* time again, eh?'

'Now you see this rope,' the Beast continued, smacking it with his switch. 'It's the quick way of getting a trooper used to the feel of a parachute descent. Back in the States they do it by means of a balloon. Here we haven't got a balloon, so we'll do it my way. Friar Tuck!'

With a groan, Lt Al Cheetham stubbed out his habitual cigar and moved forward.

'Well, man, what are you waiting for?' the Beast snapped. 'Show them how it works and let's get this show on the road!'

Friar Tuck bent down and pulling his grey habit up, tied it into a kind of large-sized nappy between his hairy thighs to reveal a pair of para-trooper boots. 'Say a prayer for me, guys,' he said merrily, and grasped the handles of the wheel supported on the wire above his head.

'Okay, this is the drill,' the Beast went on. 'You'll go down that slide at an ever-increasing speed. When you're ten yards from the pole over there, I shall order "go". When you hear that command, *drop*! Because if you don't, you're going to run smack into the pole – and you wouldn't want that, would you?'

For a moment Otto thought the Beast was going to smile, but he was wrong, though it was obvious that the thought of a trainee being smashed by impact with the pole was a pleasant one. 'Are we certain you'll give that command?' he asked.

'Shut up!' the Beast barked. 'All right, Friar Tuck. Ready?'

'Ready!'

'Move out!'

Friar Tuck launched himself over the edge of the gorge with a hefty push of his muscular legs. Immediately he started to descend along the wire, whizzing downwards at an ever increasing speed, the wire singing shrilly as the pulley soared across it.

'*GO!*' the Beast yelled through his loud-hailer.

Friar Tuck dropped, curling himself into a tight grey

ball, skirts flying to reveal bare buttocks, before he struck the hard ground in a flurry of grey dust.

'*Jesus, Maria, Josef!*' the Count cried in fear and crossed himself. 'Have we got to do *that*?'

'You do,' the Beast said and slapped his cane against his thigh, '*now!*' He licked his thin cruel lips. 'If you don't, you will be punished for refusing an order. After all, it's just like jumping off a high cliff. Nothing to it.'

'Naturally,' Otto said ironically. 'Nothing to it.' But as always irony was wasted on the Beast. 'I really enjoy falling off cliffs . . .'

Thus they trained all that day until their bodies were a mass of bruises and their hands and knees black with caked dried blood. Finally, however, as the burning sun started to slide over the yellow horizon and the stark black shadows of the night began to race rapidly over the burning desert, the Beast relented and called a halt to the day's work, adding before he strode off to his tent, eager presumably for another session with one of his Arab boys. 'Tomorrow we do it for real, guys.'

Later the two comrades sat in front of their tent, cooking their corned beef stew over a desert fire made by pouring petrol into a tin can filled with sand. Their worn faces seeming even more hollow in the flickering blue flame as they listened to husky-voiced Lala Andersen singing her nostalgic song from *Soldatensender Belgrad*[1]. The *Afrika Korps* for which it had been intended had long vanished from Africa but still the song had its old nostalgic effect on Otto as he stirred the stew with his knife. Her voice seemed to reach out to him and made him feel just how far away he was from his homeland, Germany.

'*Unter der Laterne,*
Vor dem grossen Tor . . .

[1] Forces Radio-Belgrade

Even the atmospheric distortion couldn't spoil that husky, sugar-sweet voice, as she lingered over the commonplace story of a young girl parted from her soldier love by the sound of the bugle outside the barracks gate.

'Count,' he said.

'Yes, Otto my boy,' his companion answered, his normally excited tones somehow subdued by the music and the desert night. 'What is it?'

Otto took his gaze from the immense velvet stretch of the desert sky, studded with the warm silver sheen of the stars. 'Do you think there is any future to this crazy scheme the Amis have dreamed up for us?' he asked quietly.

'I know what you mean, Otto,' the Count answered with unusual sobriety for a man so given to self-dramatization. 'Most Europeans would think the Americans crazy, but they are an amazing people. They ignore the difficulties unlike us Europeans. That's perhaps why they often succeed in what we would regard as impossible situations.'

'Impossible, that is the operative word, Count,' Otto said, gently stirring the stew as Lala Andersen came to the end of her song. From the unlit tent among the palms came the regular thwack-thwack of the Beast's cane. 'But to attempt to convince a German divisional commander to attack a tough target when he's got a soft American—'

'Soft American?' Friar Tuck's cheerful voice cut into Otto's words, as the plump OSS Lieutenant entered the small circle of flickering blue light. 'Now you wouldn't call *that* soft, would you?' he jerked his thumb at the Beast's tent. 'That's real discipline for you.'

Otto grinned and indicated that Friar Tuck should sit down. 'Want a bowl of corned beef stew, Friar?' he asked. 'Made from genuine old men.'

Friar Tuck shook his head. 'How common! I've just had cous-cous and fried sheep's balls with Arabs. You know we Americans have exquisite taste – in all things.'

Otto grinned again and taking the Count's dixie ladled some of the stew into it, as the American produced a flask of Algerian brandy and started pouring three canteen cups of the fiery spirit. 'Make your hair curl,' he grunted. 'And you're gonna need it, because fellahs, it's tomorrow.'

'What's tomorrow?' the Count asked with his mouth full of hot stew.

'The jump?'

'You mean the practice drop?'

Friar Tuck hesitated only a fraction of a second. 'There's been a snafu. There's gonna be no further training. We're gonna drop over Sicily tomorrow night.' He drained his brandy.

'*Tomorrow night!* Without training?' the Count gasped in horror.

'They're going to give us a parachute though, your friends, the amazing Americans,' Otto mocked.

The Count wasn't listening; he was too shocked by Friar Tuck's surprise announcement. 'But what happened?' he spluttered. 'Why?'

'Montgomery has rumbled that there's something up. Our spies at his HQ tell us that he's sicced one of his own counter-espionage guys on to us, a Colonel Blackie Burrows. He's supposed to be one of their wizards, old hand at the spy game, worked at it all over the jolly old Empire and that sort of thing. 'Friar Tuck's grin vanished. 'At all events, ole Blood an' Guts wants to see us tomorrow morning to give us his own personal blessing, I suppose, and then fellahs, we're off.' Friar Tuck rose to his feet. 'Enjoy your supper – and pleasant dreams.'

With that he vanished into the purple gloom leaving Otto and the Count staring at each other, spoons at their lips, as if frozen into position for all eternity like third-rate actors at the end of a fourth-rate play.

Over in the palms the Arab boy shrieked.

' "Ape the wily Pathan", what Carruthers?' Colonel

'Blackie' Burrows whispered from where the two of them lay on the edge of the oasis and lowered his night glasses.

Carruthers, his young assistant, did the same and the blue glow of the camp fire disappeared. Now there was no sound save that of the desert wind, the strange rustling sound made by millions of grains of sand contracting in the night coolness, and far away that continuous thwack-thwack.

Together with his CO Carruthers 'aped the wily Pathan' and wriggled back out of sight behind the warm dune of sand. There he waited for his chief's pronouncement on the events witnessed that day in this remote oasis.

'Blackie' Burrows was dressed, as was his custom on such assignments, in native robes complete with head-dress; what Carruthers scathingly called, behind his back, 'his sodding old Lawrence of Arabia gear'; the fact that he also wore spurs and boots and the old honey-coloured puttees of the Indian Army seemed slightly out of place. Nor could he speak a word of Arabic, but insisted on addressing any local they met in Urdu, which left most of them very puzzled.

'Never underrate the wily Pathan, Carruthers,' Burrows broke the heavy silence at last. 'Never on the North-West Frontier at least. Strip themselves bollock-naked they would and grease their bodies and slip into our quarters like snakes. Woe betide the chappies who hadn't locked up their bondooks. They'd be off with the rifles before you could say Jack Robinson.' He guffawed softly.

'Yes sir, quite sir,' Carruthers answered dutifully though he was completely at a loss as to what this had to do with those mysterious Yanks out there who had spent the long hot day playing some fool kid's game with a wire slide. 'All very strange, sir, don't you think?' Carruthers said, unable to wait any longer.

'You think so, what?' Blackie asked tugging at the end of his long nose and inadvertently rubbing off some of the brown face powder he used for his Lawrence of Arabia guise.

'Yes, I suppose I do, sir,' the younger officer replied dutifully. 'I think it's funny that a couple of Yanks come to this remote place to watch a middle-aged buffer and a younger chap, both apparently civilians, playing kids' games? I also think it's funny that the two civvies spoke German together on two occasions.'

'Damned cunning old Johnny Pathan, you know, Carruthers.'

Over at the tented area, the caning sounds had ended and given way to muffled sobbing, whether of delight or pain, Carruthers couldn't tell. All he wished at this moment was that he was back in the mess, showered and shaved and wrapping himself around several ice-cold whisky and sodas.

'Now the slide-business,' Blackie said. 'You don't know what that is for, do you? I'll tell you. It's a way of training para-troopers, that's what it is.'

'Training paras out here, sir? But what on earth for?'

Blackie didn't seem to hear, instead he said, 'And then this business of the two civvies speaking Boche. What do you think that means? They *are* Boche, of course!'

Carruthers groaned. 'Excuse me, sir, but I really don't think I'm cut out for Intelligence. I should have stayed with the Cherrypickers.[1] Life was so simple in the desert.'

'Don't take on, laddie. You've never fought against the wily Pathan as I have. It's the best kind of training for the Great Game, you know. Well, to sum up – what have we got, eh?'

'Well, sir, we've got Yanks training a couple of Huns how to jump from an aeroplane in the middle of nowhere,' Carruthers answered a little hopelessly.

'Exactly, my boy. So?'

'So, I give up, sir. What does it all mean?'

'Pity a chap can't light up out here. I could do with a

[1] The 11th Hussars

pipe o' baccy at the moment. Helps the old thought-processes, you know.'

'Do you mean *you* don't know either, sir?'

'Of course!' Blackie snorted. 'Just testing your powers of reason, young chap.'

'Sorry, sir.'

'Think nothing of it. I say, have you taken the parachute course yet, Carruthers?' The sudden change of subject surprised the younger officer.

'N-no sir? I've been out in the Western Desert since '40. When I was training back in the UK they didn't have a parachute regiment.'

Blackie absorbed the information and Carruthers, not only totally bewildered but suddenly anxious, watched his CO's wrinkled face with apprehension.

'I shall have to report to Monty. Bit of a little bounder, I suppose, but he does get things done.'

'What things, sir?' Carruthers ventured hesitantly.

'Things like procuring us an aeroplane, Carruthers.'

'But whatever for, sir?'

'Because wherever those Boche chaps go, we go too.'

'But why, sir?' Carruthers protested. 'I mean our brief was only to—'

'Now no belly-aching, Carruthers. You're just like the Pathan you are – a damned trouble-maker.' He beamed in the darkness at his subordinate. 'Why you should be thrilled at the prospect, Carruthers. This is the Great Game, you know. Mystery, adventure, excitement, and all that sort of thing.' He rose to his feet and drew the edge of his cloak over the lower half of his face dramatically, 'Come on, young feller. No time to waste. *Back to the camels!*'

FIVE

General Patton slapped the map with his knuckles. 'Enna,' he barked, 'this is the Eyetie Headquarters. Now here to the south of Enna between Piazza Amerina and the Catania Plain lies the Hermann Goering, the best the Krauts have in the whole of the Southern Mediterranean, and it don't take any goddam crystal ball to figure out that it's those Krauts who are going to stop my Seventh when it lands down here – at Licata, Gela and Vittoria, unless this Baron guy switches his attention to the Limeys at Pachino or Cassibile – here and here.'

His listeners, Friar Tuck, the Beast, and Sergeant Carlo, for once not flicking his quarter up and down, nodded their understanding, while the Count and Otto, preoccupied with the fact that they were going to have to jump out of an aeroplane that day, looked worried.

'I can use those Krauts like the Pope can use a pecker – Oh Gosh!' Patton clapped his hand to his mouth and put on his Little-Country-Boy-Caught-with-His-Hand-in-the-Pickle-Jar Face. 'I've just blasphemed, haven't I, Red?'

Roaring Red, who was an Irish Catholic, took off his beloved helmet and looked reverently at the ceiling. 'I guess so, General, but I think the Big Sky Pilot up there will forgive you. It's the strain and stress of command, General.'

'Thank you, Red,' Patton said, apparently genuinely relieved. 'Well back to the mission. Intelligence had first thought you should be dropped here, close to Caltagirone, which they think is the Hermann Goering HQ. But now, being Intelligence, they've decided that's too risky.' Patton pointed to the south-western part of the island. 'They now believe that here near Butera, about twenty miles from the coast, is the best spot. It's being held by the Livorno Division, a collection of wop farmboys according to our information – not the world's greatest soldiers.' He sniffed. 'So, our people think it would be safer for you to jump there tonight. Red here will fill you in later on the details. Now there are just two other things I wish to talk to you guys about before you go. Monty, somehow or other, has gotten on to us. He pokes that goddam long nose of his into everything, so you've got to be God-awful careful. If this came out, there'd be one sweet hell of a scandal. Clear?'

His American listeners nodded their heads dutifully.

'The second point, gentlemen, is this,' Patton continued. 'I am now going to reveal the date of D-Day to you and thus you now become what are officially known as *bigots*. It will be tenth July, 1943.' He stared around at their set faces, his own features set in his Leader of Men Number Two Look. 'As bigots, gentlemen, you should – again officially – go nowhere near the front in case you might be captured. Now, if you *are* captured, you will under no circumstances reveal what you know. Do you understand that? Even if they torture you, your lips must remain sealed to the very end.'

Captain Wipem's eyes gleamed with sudden excitement. 'You can rely on us, General,' he said enthusiastically. 'Me and the boys know all about pain, don't we guys?'

Friar Tuck grinned. 'I suppose *you* could say that, Captain,' he agreed.

'Good, gentlemen, now would you please kneel,' Patton commanded.

Near the window Red Rory again took off his precious helmet and went down on one knee and a bewildered, red-faced Otto found himself forced to do likewise as General Patton's craggy features slipped into his Visionary Man-of-God Look. He raised his cold grey eyes to the ceiling and

THE SITUATION IN SICILY, JULY 1943

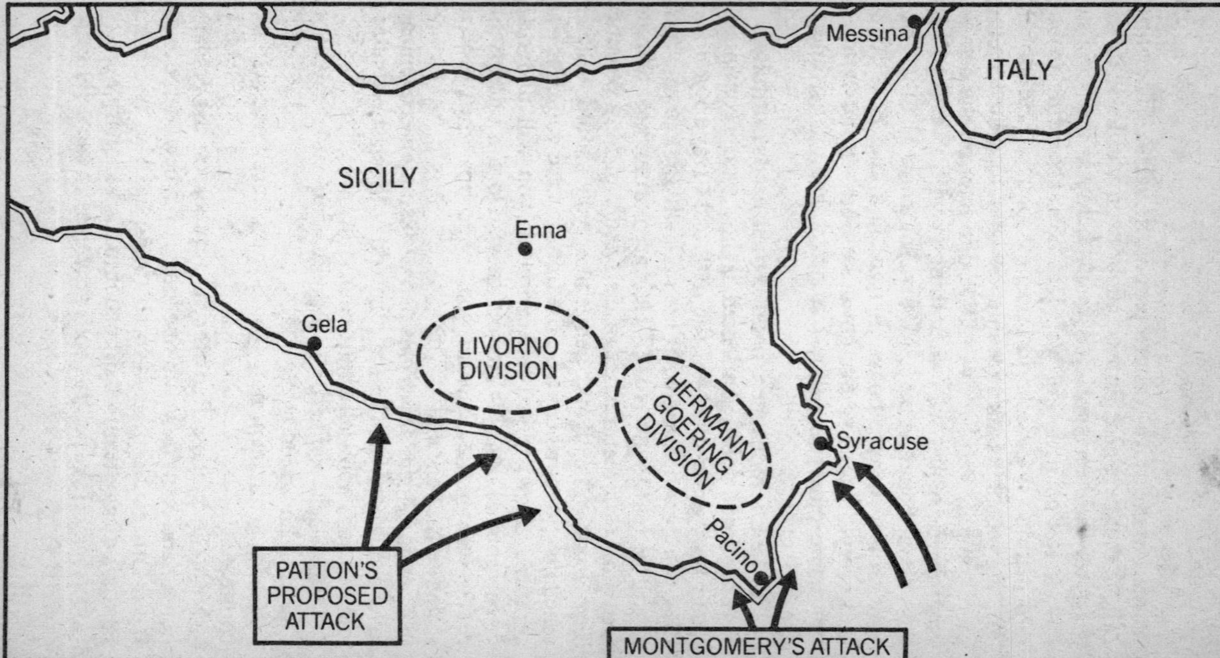

commenced in the sing-song tones of an Episcopalian clergyman of one of New York's richer churches, 'O Lord of Hosts, listen to this my prayer.'

Otto gasped. The General was praying – *to God!*

'We Americans are a competitive race. Soon we are going to enter the greatest sporting competition of all time – battle. God of our Father who by land and by sea has led us into victory, please continue Your Inspiring Guidance in this the newest of our conflicts.'

Otto stole a surreptitious glance at the faces of his companions. Naturally the Count's glowed with instant holiness; it was typical of him and to be expected. But the Americans looked similarly pious, no trace of humour on their deathly serious faces; even the Beast seemed to have succumbed to the piety of the mood. Otto shook his head in wonder; the Amis certainly were a strange people, very strange indeed!

'Strengthen my soul so that the weakening instinct of self-preservation which besets all of us in battle shall not blind me to my duty – my own manhood, the glory of my calling and my responsibility to my fellow soldiers.' Patton sucked in breath respectfully, and continued. 'Smite mine enemies O Lord, God Our Father, and ensure mine rival, the General of the English, B. L. Montgomery shall not gain the victory in the coming conflict. Please maketh possible that Thine humble servant George S. Patton Junior shall reach the citadel of Messina. I beseech Thee.' And then the sing-song affectation disappeared from Patton's voice to be replaced by a pleading note of naked greed. 'Give me Messina, O Lord!'

The heavy brooding silence which ensued was broken by Red Rory's solemn 'amen' as he crossed himself.

'Amen', intoned the others and the Beast, so carried away by Patton's impromptu prayer, even forgot to slap his boot with his cane.

Stiffly they rose to their feet. Patton took his eyes off the flaking ceiling which had ceased to be a celestial cloud with an old man with a long white beard sitting on it listening to the prayer of his 'humble servant' George S. Patton, and had become a ceiling once more. Patton grinned, his face breaking into his Cheeky Andy Hardy Look Number One.

'All right, fellers,' he chirped enthusiastically in his high-pitched voice, 'what yer waiting for? You've got God on your side now. *Let's root hog . . .!*'

The Dakota ploughed steadily through the warm summer night. The steady drone of its engines had induced sleep in the Americans and now all three of them snored open-mouthed in the bucket seats. Even the crew chief who was in charge of the drop sawed wood happily on a pile of blankets to the rear of the plane.

Otto watched them bitterly. 'Look at the shits, Count,' he grumbled. 'How in three devils' name can they sleep at a moment like this?'

As usual the Count was lost to reality, as if he had completely forgotten the hazardous undertaking which lay ahead. 'They are so young, Otto. You must understand. They need the sleep,' he said soothingly.

'What about shitting Mrs Stahl's handsome son?' Otto exploded indignantly. 'I'm young too! I need the shut-eye as well! But do you think I'm gonna get it, thinking all the time that in thirty minutes or so, I'm going to step out of this bit of metal and canvas and start walking on air – at two thousand metres up? Christ, who do you think I am, eh?'

'I should imagine it will be an interesting experience, Otto,' the Count said mildly.

'Oh yes, getting yer dong caught in a wringer is also an interesting experience, but it's something that I, for one, could well do without. I'm gonna—'

He stopped short. There was a sudden tapping noise on the right side of the Dakota, as if some gigantic bird had rapped on the fabric with its beak, and the plane suddenly swung fifty metres into the air, leaving Otto's stomach somewhere far behind. 'What in hell's name was that?' he croaked in alarm, as the others started to wake up.

'It's okay, fellers,' the cheerful second pilot, who looked all of thirteen with his freckled innocent face and fur cap stuck to the back of his tousled blond head called from up front, while his companion fought to right the plane. 'Just a little flak. The Wops are lousy shots. You see we're crossing the coast now where they've got their main batteries! Nothing to worry about . . .'

The words died on his lips as the pilot threw the plane violently to the left and a sudden line of holes, letting in jets of cold air, appeared along the length of the fuselage.

'The Wops are lousy shots, eh,' Otto said thickly. 'They must have been getting in some practice of late.'

'Don't worry, Otto,' Friar Tuck said, waking up with a huge yawn, 'we'll soon be nice and safe on terra firma.'

Otto looked at him. 'It's the bit in between that I'm worried about, friend,' he said grimly.

'All right,' the Beast said, 'knock off that talking.' With a jerk of his head, he indicated the sudden red warning light which had flashed on just over the exit door, 'five minutes to go to the DZ[1].'

The crew chief stumbled across their feet and attaching himself by his safety harness to the fuselage, leaned forward and with all his strength pushed open the door.

Immediately the plane was flooded with cold air and the deafening noise of the twin engines. By craning his neck, Otto could just see the Italian searchlights cutting the dark sky and the angry red glow of the anti-aircraft guns. He shuddered violently, at the thought of what he would have to do.

'A louse run across your liver, Otto?' the Count queried.

'Something like that,' Otto said, trying to sound nonchalant.

[1] Dropping Zone

'Hook up!' the Beast roared above the noise of the engines.

Obediently they rose and fastened the hooks at the end of their parachute straps to the wire running the length of the aircraft, securing them with split pins.

To their front the red light had changed to green. The crew chief called 'Close up!'

The five of them shuffled closer to one another with the Beast in the lead.

'Action stations – Number One!' the crew chief bellowed.

The Beast moved to the door, poised there in a half-crouch, hands gripping the panels at both sides, the wind tugging violently at his clothes.

'*Go!*' the crew chief screamed.

The Beast let go. It was almost as if the wind had reached up and dragged him out of the aircraft. Otto shuddered and closed his eyes. The Beast had actually jumped! That proved he was crazy. Anyone who was prepared to do something like that would have to be crazy.

'Number Two!' the crew chief's harsh voice broke into his thoughts. Before him the dark-eyed Sergeant shuffled to the door.

'*Go!*'

Once again the wind seemed to reach in and pluck him from the door. In an instant he had vanished.

'Number Three!'

It was him! Suddenly he was bathed in a cold sweat, his legs felt like rubber, his heart beat frantically.

'Go on, Otto,' Friar Tuck behind him urged. 'Just don't think about it. Do as the crew chief orders.'

Blindly Otto stumbled forward.

'*Go!*' the crew chief roared, and he went.

He had a split-second's impression of the plane's tail above him and the scarlet spurts of flame from the engine exhausts lighting the darkness. Momentarily he was buffeted to and fro by the slipstream. Then he was falling through the night at a tremendous rate. Panic overcame him. He screamed. The chute wasn't going to open. He was plunging to his death, his body would be smashed to pulp.

Above him there was a sharp crack. White silk mushroomed above him and the terrifying descent was braked, as the parachute bellied out and became a creamy silent canopy above his head.

For a few seconds he felt wretched as the chute moved back and forth, swinging him from horizontal to vertical. And then the chute righted itself and he was overcome by a wonderful sensation of peace, silence and relief as he floated downwards. 'Holy strawsack,' he muttered in delight, 'I've done it – jumped out of an aeroplane with a bit of knicker silk to hold me up!'

But Otto's delight was short-lived. For as the ground loomed up ever larger and the countryside, like a patchwork quilt bathed in the icy light of the stars, became clearly visible, he saw to his horror that he was fast approaching the centre of a large lake or reservoir. Desperately he pulled at the shroud-lines, frantically trying to recall what Friar Tuck had told him about guiding a parachute. And then remembering the canopy could act as a kind of sail he tried to gauge the direction of the wind, and pulled down the lift webs.

It worked. He started to skim across the silver gleaming surface of the water like a yacht. Twice his toes ducked under and he thought the canopy would collapse and drop him right into the lake, but both times his luck held out and then, as his desperate gaze caught the first glimpse of a wood of stunted olive trees, the chute did fold. He dropped straight down. The silk hit the water – and Otto the bank. He had done it with millimetres to spare.

What followed was a frantic fumbling to free himself from the shrouds, a hurried scraping away of the damp earth of the embankment to bury his chute, and a mad scampering to the edge of the wood.

There was no sign of the others. Above him the starry heavens were empty and the only sound was the soft rustle of the night breeze in the stunted olives. Cautiously Otto depressed the little toy which the Beast had given him just before take-off. It gave off a sound like the croak of a bull-frog and it was their agreed-upon recognition signal. It seemed deafening to him and for a moment he had visions of hordes of excited Italian soldiers coming rushing at him from out of the trees. Nothing of the sort happened. All he received in way of a reply to his signal was the angry hoot of some night-owl.

He tried it again.

Again nothing!

Otto frowned and sat down. His method of escape from drowning in the lake had carried him well away from the others – that was obvious now. It was also obvious that he was somewhere in the middle of Sicily with a large American pistol strapped under his shoulder and his pockets bulging with American dollars. It wouldn't take even the stupidest village cop to figure out that he was up to no good, no good at all.

He stood up. Still all was silence. He frowned. 'Otto my lad,' he said to himself grimly, 'it seems to me that you've gone and got yourself up to your hooter in shit once again.'

SIX

The night breeze was not strong, but strong enough to move Carlo's body back and forth as it hung there grotesquely from the tree by the parachute harness. Carlo had broken his neck. Now he hung there as if on a gibbet.

But the others crouching in the rustling brush had no eyes for that eerie sight; for now they could hear the soldiers beating the ground to their front quite clearly. Like all Italians they made too much noise.

'To the right,' Friar Tuck whispered to the Beast, easing out his silenced Colt ·45. 'Two o'clock, beyond that clump of olives, Wipem!'

The Beast grunted his assent and drew his pistol. Behind the two Americans the Count shivered, the fact that this was a great adventure forgotten for the moment in face of the impending danger.

Now silhouetted a stark black against the silver sheen of the stars, they could see six or seven searchers, rifles slung carelessly over their shoulders while they beat the undergrowth with tree branches, shouting noisily to one another as they advanced up the little slope in a ragged line.

'They probably think we're shot-down air crew or something,' the Beast whispered contemptuously. 'Easy pickings.' He curled his finger round the trigger of his heavy silenced Colt. 'Those dagoes are gonna be in for a surprise.'

'But you can't kill them all!' Friar Tuck objected. 'Besides if you did, they'd be missed and the whole damned countryside would be out looking for them.'

'Have you got an alternative?' the Beast asked with a sneer.

'Yes,' Friar Tuck snapped, his usual good-humour vanished. It seemed to him that the mission was going badly wrong – and they'd scarcely started. First they'd lost Carlo, then Otto. Now the Eyeties had got on to them right away. 'Let 'em find poor old Carlo up there. That should keep them happy. And who knows they might even decide to call off the search.'

'But what happens when they search the body and find the greenbacks, his pistol and ID?' the Beast objected. 'Then they'll really be cooking with gas.'

'Maybe,' Friar Tuck shrugged carelessly. 'But by that time we'll be well on our way. By hook or by crook we'll get ourselves some wheels and put a helluva lot of distance between us and here.'

'I agree with you, young man,' the Count spoke for the first time, 'I know the southern mentality. There'll be endless discussions about the corpse and by the time they are prepared to act, we will be long gone.'

The Beast considered for a moment, while the body squeaked back and forth eerily to their front and the Italian soldiers came ever closer. 'All right,' he said in the end, 'let's do it your way. But I sure as hell hate to let those Wops get away with it. They're just sitting ducks down there.'

'Later on, I'll let you stick pins in yourself – as a reward,' Friar Tuck sneered. 'Come on, let's make it, while there's still time.'

The Count needed no urging. He started to back deeper into the trees, heavy with the scent of resin and wild honeysuckle. Friar Tuck followed and then, reluctantly, the Beast.

Five minutes later the Italians discovered the dead body of the American sergeant. The night silence was broken by the excited chatter of their voices as they poked at the corpse and tugged at its feet in an attempt to dislodge it until finally two of them released it by climbing the tree and cutting the shroud lines.

'Cruel bastards . . . no respect for the dead,' Friar Tuck whispered.

'Cruelty has its uses,' the Beast hissed back, eyes narrowed to slits, as he watched the Italians organize themselves into a bearer party to transport the corpse away. 'Anyway, you were right, Cheetham. They're obviously calling off the search. Look.'

Dimly they could see the diminutive Italian soldiers placing the dead body on their shoulders, arms linked as a primitive stretcher beneath it, and beginning to stagger awkwardly down the hillside with their burden.

They watched them disappear and waited five minutes before they set off in the opposite direction with the Beast in the lead. Exactly one hour later they ran straight into the road block. The group of men in dark civilian clothes who stood there, seemed to have been expecting them.

'*Ovra!*' their leader snapped and pushed a silver badge under the Beast's surprised gaze.

Before he even had time to think of his pistol other civilians carrying machine-pistols had started to emerge from the dark shadows, surrounding them. The three men were trapped.

Slowly and miserably the Count and Friar Tuck started to raise their hands. There was nothing else they could do . . .

The big open touring car nearly caught Otto by surprise as it swung round the corner of the dusty little road in the grey light of dawn and came tearing towards him, headlights blazing.

Otto reacted quickly. He whipped open his flies and pretended to be urinating against the nearest tree, though his bowels were so taut and tied-up that he could not have made water if his very life had depended upon it.

The big car came level with him. In the front seat a dark little man with a large broad-brimmed hat that made him look like a gangster in a Hollywood movie wagged his finger in admonishment and then, as the speeding tyres wreathed him in dust, he caught a quick glimpse of the Count's face set in tragic fortitude. Next instant the car was gone careering up the rough road towards the little town which clung seemingly fearfully to the hillside in the far distance as if it was about to fall off.

Otto whistled softly and buttoned up his flies. The civilians, who were obviously plain clothes bulls, had the Count and probably the Americans too. The silly fart had gone and got himself captured straight off. Otto bit his bottom lip as he watched the black car disappear from view. What was he going to do?

He stood there staring at the little clinging hillside township for a long while until the call of roosters heralding the new dawn alerted him to the danger of standing around. He knew it would be foolish to attract attention, so he made a quick decision. He'd have a look at the town. With a sigh, he set off up the road, as the sun popped up like a red clay-pigeon and banished the morning cool. Within minutes that dusty plain seemed to ring like metal under the impact of its brilliant white light . . .

One hour later, his face lathered with sweat, Otto was plodding wearily past the first miserable houses at the edge of the town. Dark-clad grannies, their toothless faces withered like a mummy's shrunken skull, sat on tiny stools outside the doors of their miserable hovels knitting busily; while naked children, their brown bellies swollen with malnutrition, played lethargically in the dirt-filled gutters. None of them so much as glanced in his direction, yet somehow he had the sensation that once he had passed they glared at his broad sturdy back, dark eyes filled with the hatred of the 'have-nots' for the 'haves'.

Otto wiped the sweat from his brow with his sleeve and told himself that not even in Russia had he seen such misery as in this Sicilian cliff-township. The houses seemed to be crumbling back to the stone from which they had been hewn centuries before. The animals, such as they were, were moth-eaten and skinny-ribbed with hardly strength enough to crop the parched grass; and the whole place stank of piss and poverty. 'Christ,' he cursed under his breath, as he turned out of a narrow stinking alley, into the main square, 'who'd live here?'

He paused in the shadows cast by one of the larger municipal buildings located in the square and took in the scene. A couple of skinny dogs panted long-tongued in the gutters. Next to the communal water-tap which bore the symbol of Mussolini's vaunted 'New Order' – the Roman bundles of rods – a little one-legged veteran of the Duce's beaten army in Africa dozed over his crutch, his tin begging-bowl empty. Over at the church, two black-shawled old women crossed themselves slowly with holy water, watched by a bored waiter at a café waiting for customers who would never come.

Otto's gaze fell on the big black open car. It was the one he had seen the Count in. As casually as he could he began to stroll the length of the square towards it, keeping to the shadows, telling himself that with his height and cropped blond hair he stuck out like a sore thumb. But there was no other way to do it.

He paused in the doorway of the church and looked in. A fat priest sprawled lazily in a pew, reading a newspaper, pausing every now and again to take greedy bites of a large hunk of bread and salami. There would be no problem with the priest, Otto thought, should he have to make a dash for it through the nave. Turning once again, he pretended to cross himself with holy water while he surveyed the place outside which the black police car was parked.

It was obviously the local jail. The Italian flag hung limply over the doorway, which was closed, unlike the rest of the doors in the square, and the flyblown windows were barred. He sucked his front teeth thoughtfully. Behind him in the dark, incense-heavy cave of the church, the fat priest had finished his sandwich and was washing it down with hefty swigs of wine straight from the bottle. 'So that's what happens to the collection money,' Otto quipped to himself, somehow pleased with the sight, and moved on. He'd have a look at the place from behind.

But he did not get that far.

'*Tedescho*,' the waiter hissed as he passed. 'German, you ficki-ficki?' The dark-faced man's German was barely intelligible, but the obscene gesture he made was clear enough.

Otto stopped in his tracks. The waiter had obviously recognized him as a German, which was hardly surprising. Perhaps off-duty German soldiers had even penetrated to this remote poverty-stricken place in search of that commodity which soldiers of all nations sought in their free time – gash. '*Ja*,' he said, speaking the same broken German as the waiter, '*ich Deutscher . . . Du – Frau?*'

The waiter gave him a tremendous smile, his black liquid Italian eyes filled with triumph, as if he personally had achieved something of great importance. '*Si, si*, German . . . Big girl, very big girl.' His dirty brown hands carved a pair of breasts of elephantine proportions in the air. 'Very warm heart!' He lowered his voice conspiratorially. 'You have money . . . coffee . . . cigarettes?'

Otto nodded, his brain racing furiously. With a bit of luck, the spaghetti-eaters would keep their prisoners in the local lock-up till dark, but he couldn't hang about in the open till then; he was too conspicuous. Hadn't the waiter spotted him immediately? He would have to lie low until it was dark enough to make an attempt to rescue the Count and the Amis, and what better place to do that than a whore's bedroom? What was it that his mother 'the Witch', who had been a pavement-pounder herself in her time, had always cautioned him? 'If you're ever on the run from the bulls, Otto, my son, allus dance a mattress polka with a pavement-pounder. They've got hearts of gold – sometimes.'

'Where is this honest whore?' he asked.

'No whore . . . Irma my sister.' The waiter broke off suddenly and his dark eyes flashed fire. *'Va fa un colo!'* he cursed. Hawking throatily, he spat angrily in the dust of the gutter.

Otto followed the direction of his gaze.

It was the man he had seen in the driving seat of the tourer. In spite of the baking heat, the under-sized Italian was dressed in a heavy cloth overcoat that reached down to his narrow, pointed patent-leather shoes with raised heels, and he had his felt hat pulled down well over his sallow pock-marked face.

'Who is he?' Otto asked, as the man disappeared into the jail.

'He pig,' the waiter snarled. 'Big, big pig. He Ovra.'

'Ovra – what's that?'

But the waiter had no time for further explanations. *'Advanti!'* he cried, propelling Otto into the dark interior of the shabby café. 'You jig-jig now. Priest, he jig-jig on Thursday evenings and Irma like be fresh for priest, 'cos he holy . . .'

'Ovra?' Friar Tuck queried, as he squatted there on the dirty straw, nursing the nasty bruise on his chin where the little cop had smashed his pistol butt against it. 'What's that when it's at home?'

'Organizzione Vigilanza Repressione Antifascismo,' the Count answered gloomily staring up at the dirty barred window and the whitewashed wall scribbled with graffiti in a dozen hands. 'A kind of Italian gestapo, if you like, though there are more criminals in it than you would find in the German organization.'

'What do you mean?' the Beast asked.

'When Mussolini formed it in the twenties in order to

fight the anti-fascists on the mainland, he enrolled the Sicilian mafia into it and transferred it across to Italy proper. It was one way of getting the Sicilian mafia under control. But of course the mafia brought their own methods with them,' the Count frowned hard, as if he had just thought of something very unpleasant.

'Methods?' Friar Tuck asked.

'Of course the usual things – beatings, torture and the like. But also a few refinements of their own. The broken knee-cap to cripple a prisoner for life. Massive doses of castor oil for obvious reasons.'

'I say,' the Beast interrupted quite cheerfully, 'I would never have thought of that one.'

Friar Tuck silenced the tall dark sadist with a frown.

'And castration,' the Count ended his gloomy litany. 'It is particularly effective with Latin people. The men do have this overweening pride in their sexual abilities.'

Friar Tuck shuddered and grabbed his flies protectively. '*Please*, Count, that's enough!' he gasped. 'But do you think they'd use those methods on us. They've got our pistols, ID and dough and they must have a pretty good idea we're American Intelligence agents. What more do they need to know before they throw us in the calaboose and fling away the key to the dungeon for good?'

'What our mission is, you fool!' the Beast said scornfully. 'And remember General Patton's last instruction? We must keep our lips sealed – otherwise the success of the whole invasion might well be in jeopardy.'

'I know, I know,' Friar Tuck said and flung a helpless glance around the dirty cell, its sole adornments a chipped enamel latrine bucket in the corner and a crucifix nailed to the wall and ringed with barbed wire, as if the authorities were afraid someone might steal it. 'Jesus H Christ, we've got to find some way of getting out of this dump before they start putting pressure on us. *We've gotta!*'

The Count cocked his head to one side and listened to the rattle of pans beyond the other wall where the secret policemen had their quarters. He glanced at his watch, which for some reason they'd let him keep. 'They will be eating soon. As you know, the Italians take their food seriously. Then they will sleep a little while and then—' he shrugged, dismay written across his fleshy handsome face.

'The fun and games will start?' Friar Tuck said.

The Count nodded.

'This is no time for despondency and defeatism,' the Beast announced, breaking the heavy silence which had followed the Count's gloomy prediction. 'We're ten times smarter than those darned guineas. We can't just sit on our duffs and let fate have its way with us. Guys,' his dark eyes blazed from his skinny dark face, 'we've got to come up with a plan – and darned quick too. Now we might have three hours before those Ovra jerks get round to questioning us. So let's have some suggestions. Let's get on the stick, eh?'

Friar Tuck looked at his superior officer sourly. '*You* get on the stick, Wipem. I'm plumb outa ideas this week . . .' He relapsed into a morose silence. There was no sound now save the frizzling noise of frying pasta next door and the hectic energetic squeaking of rusty bedsprings from the dingy inn across the street – a strange unexpected sound in this remote decaying township . . .

SEVEN

'You lika tits, Otto?' Irma, the waiter's sister asked, ogling the naked weary German yet again and thrusting out her voluminous breasts at him, as if she intended to gouge out his eyes with the sharp, pink-tipped nipples. Otto backed off and the old brass-bound bedstead squeaked noisily.

Down below the old granny who owned the *albergo* rammed her stick against the low ceiling furiously although Guido, Irma's waiter-brother, had said she was as deaf as a post and wouldn't hear a thing.

'Granny's angry,' Otto said a little desperately, backing away from the whore. '*Molto furioso*, Irma.'

Irma's plump, homely features contorted into that look of contemptuous scorn she had copied from one of the actresses she had seen on one of her monthly trips to the Palermo cinema. 'The old one is jealous. No,' she slid her thumb between her two forefingers, 'no *that* for forty year. She jealous of beautiful Irma.' Again she threatened to engulf Otto's face in those breasts of hers, the white flesh gleaming with the sweat of their last coupling, as if greased with vaseline.

'Yes, yes,' Otto agreed hastily. 'But don't you think you should get ready for the priest, Irma?' He stammered in broken German. 'Priest important man.'

She puffed out her cheeks contemptuously. 'Priest, he got thing like this.' She held her forefinger and thumb about a millimetre apart. 'No good for Irma. But he priest. In Sicily everybody must obey priest.' She made another grab for Otto's naked loins. 'Irma must have real one before he come. Ha, ha!' she laughed suddenly, exhibiting her precious gold teeth, 'before he *come*! Joke, ha, ha!'

Wearily Otto agreed, but his mind was furiously trying to come up with a rescue plan to get his comrades out of the jail opposite. 'You say everybody must obey priest, Irma?' he asked suddenly, a dim plan beginning at last to enter into the further recesses of his mind.

'*Si, si*,' she agreed. '*Molto importante*, everybody obey priest.' At his loins her plump hands were pulling at his flaccid organ as if she were milking a cow.

'Policemen too?' he queried, wincing as one of her massive breasts smashed into his right cheek.

'Policemen, barmen, farm-men – *tutto*,' she hissed, her breath coming in short hectic gasps, her eyes fixed hypnotically on the thing which was now beginning to emerge from between her pudgy white hands like a shy young red fox.

'Even these . . . er Ovra fellows?' he asked hesitantly, as the plan started to take on a definite aggressive shape.

'*Si, si, Ovra*,' she panted fervently, her white heavy breasts hanging down like tethered barrage balloons.

'Irma, will you help me?' Otto cried, as she gripped him ever more fiercely, her dark eyes seemingly about to pop out of her head with excitement.

'Anything,' she breathed. '*Anything?*'

'Then will you help me—' the rest of his request was smothered in hot sweating flesh as, beside herself with sexual frenzy, Irma gripped his hair as if his head were some kind of hand mop, and smashed his face into the gorge formed by her breasts . . .

'Okay, you guys, don'ta you try to shita me!' the big Ovra secret policeman announced in the flat harsh accent of the Bronx. 'Before de Feds deport me, I liva in the States tena years. I know de Americans.' He glared at the three prisoners with his dark suspicious eyes and then stabbed out a forefinger like a blunt-ended pork sausage at Friar

Tuck and rasped, 'You, whatya dressed like a dame for, eh? You some kinda fairy, eh?'

Even when faced with this angry giant of a secret policeman who had New York hood written all over his ugly, broken-nosed face, Lieutenant Al Cheetham could not resist expressing his pride in his cover. 'Of course not,' he replied indignantly, 'this is my habit. I'm a friar.' The cop gave an ugly snicker. 'Then say the Act of Contrition,' he demanded.

For a moment Friar Tuck was caught off guard, but he recovered quickly enough. 'I can't,' he answered. 'I'm not that kind of friar. I'm . . . er . . . Episcopalian.'

'Yeah, piss you are . . . *a piss-poor liar!*' the cop sneered. 'Now listen to a me. My chief knows who you are. You're dangerous American agents, spies every one of ya.' He glared around at their pale faces and the Count quavered at the angry look. He had always thought of the Italians as an easy-going, gentle nation, but this Ovra giant looked anything else but easy-going and gentle. He suspected the man could resort to violence at the drop of a hat. 'All he don't know is why you come here to Sicily. But, friends, he's soon gonna find out.' The cop grinned evilly, ''Cos you guys are gonna sing, ain't ya, sing like da canaries?'

The Beast shot a warning look at the others and snapped icily, 'I demand that we be regarded as legitimate prisoners-of-war and be treated according to the rules of the Geneva Convention.'

'You – demand!' the cop exploded. 'Who da hell do you thinka you are *to demand*, American prick!' His big paw moved swiftly and the Beast reeled back clutching his face, crying in alarm, 'You hit me!'

'Ya don't say,' the big cop sneered. 'I guess my mitt must have slipped.' He looked at the Count with that calculating look of the bully seeking the weakest link, the one which would snap first. 'You,' he rasped, 'whata your name?'

'They call me the Count,' the middle-aged German quavered.

'Count, eh,' the cop ran his tongue around the word, as if he was actually savouring a taste. 'You must be a big shot, yeah?'

'No, no,' the Count answered, knowing he was in trouble now, for the cop's eyes had narrowed to menacing slits, 'I'm just an ordinary fellow, a nobody really.'

'Then come here *nobody*!' Again the cop's hand shot out. Before the Count could back off, his two fingers had seized his somewhat prominent nose in a fierce grip. Enjoying every instant of it, the cop, his big blue jaw clenched, twisted the nose. The Count howled with sheer agony and fell to his knees.

'Okay, Count, singa like da canary,' the cop grunted, 'or I tear the schnozz off'n you!'

But that wasn't to be. In that very same instant the big rusty lock clicked open and the heavy timber door squeaked. 'Dino,' a harsh voice commanded, '*basta . . . pronto!*'

The cop let go of the Count's nose and he reeled back, groaning miserably, touching the organ gingerly, as if it was on fire. Then the door opened to reveal the little Ovra chief standing there, still wearing his ankle-length coat and broad-brimmed felt hat, dwarfed by a tall young man in the ill-fitting robes of a priest.

The Beast opened his mouth and then shut it quickly. A light of hope gleamed in Friar Tuck's eyes. Kneeling on the dirty floor, the Count blinked through his tears, hardly daring to believe the evidence of his own eyes.

'The Father here is from German HQ,' the Ovra man explained in reasonable German, presumably for the priest's sake. 'Our German comrades want him to give the spies a blessing before they are shot.' He flashed the big priest a winning smile.

Hands crossed piously across his chest, the priest whispered, 'It's the tragedy of war, my son. But it must be done.'

Dino, the big cop, stared at the priest surlily and said in Italian. 'What we want with a *tedeschi* bible-thumper,

Signor Capitano? We've got enough of the fornicating bastards ourselves.'

Imperiously the little Ovra chief held up his hand. 'Enough, Dino!' he commanded, 'I have spoken. As the Duce says, he who will command, must first learn to obey!' He turned to the priest and flashed him a gleaming smile – he seemed to have more teeth than most people. 'But, Father, could you tell me how your HQ became aware of these prisoners?'

The priest's pious look did not change. 'We have our ways, Captain,' he said in a soft modest voice. 'We thought in accordance with our well-known German trait of humanitarianism that they should be offered the blessing of our Holy Church before—' He did not finish the sentence. Instead he lowered his eyes and gazed mutely at his boots peeping out from beneath the too-short robe.

'Of course, of course,' the Captain agreed. 'Our German comrades are well-known for their sentimentality.' He threw out his pigeon chest and jutted his weak jaw as if he were the Duce himself speaking to the throng from his balcony in the capital. 'We Romans are of a different breed,' he said proudly. 'Hard and unyielding and—' He broke off as Dino tugged his sleeve and snapped angrily, 'What is it, son-of-a-whore?'

Mutely the big policeman gestured at the priest's boots and then at those of Friar Tuck.

'Well, what is it?' he demanded, noting that the priest did indeed wear unusual boots for his calling. They were made of excellent leather and were laced high above the ankles – they were brown too which was uncommon. Most priests wore shabby black boots in Sicily, even the Cardinal in Palermo.

'The boots,' Dino said excitedly, a dark threatening look seeping into his eyes. 'They both wear the same sort of boots.'

'So?'

'So, they're para—' The big cop reeled against the wall

as Otto slammed the little Captain into him. Friar Tuck needed no urging to take part in the proceedings; he had a score to pay back. 'Okay, you Wop bastard,' he growled, 'this is for the pistol whipping!' his big fist slammed into the little Captain's face. Something snapped and the Captain staggered backwards, spitting out teeth, his dazzling white smile vanished for ever.

Otto had cornered the big cop before he could protect himself, and dealt him a tremendous blow on the side of his head with his pistol butt. The cop slammed against the wall and cross-eyed, slid slowly to the ground where he crumpled into an untidy unconscious heap.

'Gee, I like your frock, Otto!' Friar Tuck cried triumphantly, as the Count and the Beast sprang forward to grab the Captain who was reeling around the cell, spitting out teeth, as if he were drunk. 'My habit looks positively dowdy against it.'

'Knock it off,' Otto said grimly, tugging the priest's robe over his head. 'There are half a dozen of the bastards out there. We've got to take them if we're going to get away with it.'

Friar Tuck grabbed the unconscious Dino's pistol out of his holster and flipped off the safety. 'Ready when you are, Otto,' he hissed.

The other two lowered the still moaning, almost unconscious Captain to the ground. The Beast snatched his pistol too and hissed as the little Italian spat out a final tooth before closing his eyes and relapsing into unconsciousness, 'And let that be a lesson to you. When people are bad they must be punished, punished—'

'Fer crying out loud,' Friar Tuck groaned, 'can't you wait till later to get your damned rocks off!'

Cautiously Otto began to edge open the cell door, gritting his teeth against the loud rusty squeak. Friar Tuck and the others peered out over his shoulder.

Sprawled out in the big dirty room were six other Italians, two of them in civilian clothes, four in uniform, but all of them wearing neat little pistols attached to their clothing somewhere or other. Beyond, the door which led out into the street was closed. If they were going to get out, they'd have to tackle the cops.

Otto held up three fingers and looked enquiringly around their tense faces to check whether they had understood. They all nodded.

Silently Otto began to mouth – one, two, *three!*

As one they burst out of the cell.

The civilian next to the door tried to rise from his chair, hand automatically fumbling for his pistol. Otto's silenced Colt jerked wildly in his hand. The slug caught the cop in the centre of his chest. His shirt suddenly flushed crimson, as he and the chair slammed into the far wall, carried there by the impact of the ·45 bullet at such close range.

Next to the cell door a uniformed policeman with a great dramatic black moustache tried to grab for Friar Tuck. Friar Tuck elbowed him cruelly in his stomach. He gasped sharply and collapsed like a suddenly deflated balloon.

Another cop tried desperately to bar their way out. The Beast's eyes gleamed in anticipation – he aimed and fired in the same instant. Once! Twice! The cop screamed, arms flailing the air wildly, as both his knee-caps shattered, bone and gore erupting in a scarlet volcano from the ruined joints. He hit the floor face-first. And then they were springing over his writhing body, wrenching open the door, and hurtling towards the parked car.

Friar Tuck ripped up his habit. With a wild scream of ecstatic abandon, carried away by the electric tension of this moment, he vaulted behind the driver's seat, followed by the others. Now scarlet stabs of flame started to cut the darkness as the surviving policemen began firing from the cover of the jail. Desperately Otto, crouched in the back seat, returned the fire, crying, 'For God's sake, get this heap started, Friar!'

'I'm trying to,' Friar Tuck cried back, fumbling with the unfamiliar controls in the glowing darkness.

'Otto, caro Otto!' a familiar voice called his name above the angry snap-and-crackle of the small arms fire.

Otto flung a wild glance upwards, as Friar Tuck cursed and fumbled.

Irma hung over her balcony like an outsized Juliet, great boobs glowing luminously in the darkness, waving frantically, *'Otto! Don't leave me!'*

'Get your silly head down—' Otto's angry reproof was cut short by a burst of submachine-gun fire. Behind him the windscreen shattered and bright gleaming holes appeared, as if by magic, the length of the car. Instinctively Otto ripped off the rest of his magazine. Someone screamed, high, shrill and Italian. *'Mama mia!'* a voice moaned.

'Screw your mama mia!' Otto yelled, his every nerve jingling electrically, as a sweating nervous Friar Tuck, his fingers feeling like clumsy thick sausages, finally found the ignition key and turned.

There was a soft miserable metallic groan.

Now the town lights were beginning to click on everywhere. Even with the submachine-gun chattering like an angry woodpecker close by, Otto could hear the heavy sound of many feet running down the dark streets bordering the *piazza*.

The Count moaned. 'We are lost . . . we're lost, Otto,' he gasped, carried away by fear, as a sweating, desperate Friar Tuck turned the key once again.

Madly Otto slammed home another magazine into the butt of the Colt and began snapping off single shots to left and right of the bullet-pocked jail-front, reasoning that the cops or anyone who wanted to stop them, would attempt to come round the rear.

The engine stirred weakly. Angrily Friar Tuck slammed his clubbed fist down on the dashboard. 'Come on, you Wop sonuvabitch, *start*, willya!'

He ripped the key back and forth once again. An air-raid siren started to wail shrilly from the roof of the municipal building opposite and the menacing sound of running feet was getting closer by the second.

'Oh, my holy arse!' Otto cried in a paroxysm of fear, 'the shits'll alert the whole of Sicily!'

Suddenly the cop with the submachine-gun burst from a side street, firing from the hip as he ran. The Beast snapped off a couple of shots. And then his pistol jammed. The cop was no more than fifty metres away now. At the driver's seat, Friar Tuck turned the key frantically to the same dull unresponding engine note. Otto took aim – he knew he had only one slug left in his magazine. If he missed, they'd be lost. They'd be slaughtered by the cop's submachine-gun. Crouched next to him, the Count began to pray.

Hardly daring to breathe, holding on to the big Colt with all his remaining strength, for he knew just how high the powerful pistol kicked, Otto fired.

For what seemed an age, nothing happened. Then suddenly, frighteningly, the cop screamed and stopped as if he had just run into a brick wall. In that very same instant the tourer's engine sprang into powerful vibrating life and the night air filled with the stink of petrol.

Disbelievingly Friar Tuck jammed home first gear, yelled, '*Here we go, fellahs!*' and they were off, speeding forward, taking the first corner crazily with a furious screech of protesting rubber – leaving behind them an angry mob and a sobbing naked Irma.

Behind her on the sagging brass bed the fat priest in his dirty underwear slowly began to come round. He rubbed the bump on the back of his bald pate and stared down at his long-johns and stockinged feet in bewilderment. Slowly, as if his head was moved by rusty springs, he turned to look at the sobbing naked Irma leaning over the balcony exhibiting all her ample charms. 'God in heaven,' he croaked, rolling his dark Italian eyes miserably, 'they've caught me *in flagrante*. I've been defrocked . . .'

Irma continued to sob.

EIGHT

They drove through the night, stopping at regular intervals while one of them shinned up the signpost to check the name of the next village by means of Friar Tuck's Zippo lighter. Gradually they worked their way through the barren hills of Central Sicily towards the plain where Baron von Borkenheim's Hermann Goering Panzer division was stationed.

Twice they narrowly avoided running into roadblocks, backing up narrow dusty roads and finding new routes through the hills to circumvent them. Once, too, they nearly bumped into a long convoy of camouflaged trucks heading south towards the coast and judged from the singing coming from the backs of the vehicles that they contained Italian soldiers.

'Wops going south,' Friar Tuck commented softly, as they waited in the darkness of a grove of scented pine trees until the last of the convoy had passed. 'Do you think that means the Eyeties have rumbled that we're gonna put in a landing in two days' time and are beefing up their coastal defences?'

'Of course not,' the Beast sneered, 'and even if they have, what can the Wops do? They're not really soldiers. Just a lot of dago tenors playing soldiers. A lot of soap-opera dagoes.'

'Those cops back there weren't playing games,' Otto commented softly, as Friar Tuck slipped home first gear and they emerged from their cover. 'They died for their country.'

Towards dawn they were finally out of the hills and

with the new day bathed in the faint pink before them, and the semicircle of the sun just peeping over the horizon as if it wondered whether or not to make a full appearance, they started to roll towards a large river, flanked on both sides by lush fields of rice paddy.

Now Friar Tuck, still behind the wheel, began to cast anxious looks at the sky and Otto knew why. The Italians back at the village could well have alerted their air force to be on the look out for the fugitives and on this limitless empty plain, the lone black tourer stuck out like a sore thumb. 'Do you think we should abandon the car, Friar?' he asked, while beside him on the back seat the Count and the Beast snored softly, oblivious to the fact that they were slowly being covered in a fine white dust from the road.

'I'd like to stick with these wheels as long as possible, Otto,' the big American replied, not taking his eyes off the narrow road with deep drainage ditches running along either side of it. 'Your all-American boy doesn't like to hoof it, you know. We're kinda delicate.' He smiled at his own face in the rear-view mirror.

'You delicate!' Otto grunted, staring at the American's massive shoulders, his muscles seeming about to rip open the grey habit at any moment. He yawned and fought the longing to close his eyes. 'All right,' he conceded, 'perhaps you're right, Friar. We're all tired, and I don't think the Count is ready for a long hike. But keep your eyes peeled. Right?'

'Roger,' Friar Tuck agreed and pressed his foot down on the accelerator once again.

Time passed. Otto allowed himself to close his eyes. 'Only five minutes,' he warned himself. 'Just five. Clear?'

He settled more comfortably in the back of the car, lulled into a pleasantly drowsy state by the snores of his companions and the hiss of the rubber tyres on the tarmac. Already the night cool had begun to vanish and the breeze which had kept him awake through the long night had been replaced by a warm wind, replete with the sweet odours of the rolling Sicilian countryside.

A jumbled kaleidoscope of the last days started to unroll before his inner eye. Patton and his faces . . . his little English rival Montgomery in his overlong shorts and floppy black beret . . . the panic of the parachute drop . . . Irma and the surprised look on the fat priest's face as Otto had leapt from the closet brandishing the chair leg . . . and then of course the terrifying Irma flashing those monstrous dugs at him, advancing upon him with them firmly upraised in her hands, intent on smothering him with that gleaming white flesh.

'Otto—'

The single word cut into his confused reverie with the sharpness of a knife.

He awoke with a start.

It was bright daylight now, the road to their front ablaze with warm yellow sunshine. On both sides in the trees the birds chirped madly. 'What is it—' He broke off. Clearly visible in the rear-view mirror, he could see the slow awkward shape of a biplane bearing down upon the car directly out of the sun. He spun round, shading his eyes against the slanting, blinding rays. 'Shit!' he gasped as he spotted the red, white and green roundel of the Italian Air Force on the strange plane's fuselage. '*Macaroni!*'

'Right in one, Otto. A Savoia recon plane to be exact,' Friar Tuck gasped, a vein beginning to tic nervously at the side of his unshaven face, his knuckles on the wheel suddenly white.

'Sorry,' Otto began, but Friar Tuck cut him short swiftly.

'Forget it, Otto!' he cried, as the biplane flew ever closer, coming down so that it followed the lone car directly as it sped along the straight white road, leaving behind it a white wake of dust. 'Wake the others. *Quick!* We're in trouble, brother!'

Quickly Otto shook the Beast and then the Count, they

began to splutter awake, and then with Colt in hand he elbowed his way round so that he could face the strange plane.

Now it was some three or four hundred metres behind the car and perhaps a couple of hundred above the road so that Otto could catch brief glances of the white blur of the pilot's face beyond the whirling radial engine.

'Twin fifty mm. machine guns,' the Beast snapped, wide awake now. 'I know the type. The Wops used them in North Africa.'

'Oh, my God, what are we going to do?' the Count quavered, wringing his hands as the biplane came closer and closer.

Behind the wheel, Friar Tuck, his eyes alternating between the road and the rear-view mirror, said, 'He'll buzz us for a start, Count. Let's see what the pilot will do after that. But all of you – get ready to bale out. *Now here he comes!*'

Suddenly the air was full of the clatter of the biplane's propellor. Otto flashed a look upwards. The sun was blotted out by the roaring plane. In an instant it was over and past them, zooming forward up the road dragging its black shadow behind it like a great evil black crow to climb high into the bright blue sky and begin to turn.

Friar Tuck snapped swiftly out of the side of his mouth, 'The bastard's spotted us!' His narrowed eyes took in the biplane as it started to level out of its curve now. 'This time he's coming in for real.'

Otto flung a glance to left and right. To their right was the river, devoid of cover. It was the same on the left. The paddy-field was green with vegetation, but it was too short for them to hide in. He grunted and sprang into the front seat next to Friar Tuck. 'See that bridge up ahead.'

Friar Tuck nodded his understanding, gaze fixed on the plane hypnotically. 'If we could make that – there's that small wood to the right of the far exit. Ditch the car and into it smartish!'

Friar Tuck surveyed the bridge swiftly. It was a typical sort of structure for that part of Sicily: a rough single-span metal structure, built in the twenties in the first flush of the new fascist regime. On both sides there was a drop of some twenty metres. He might survive a drop over the side into the water, providing the river wasn't too shallow. Otto and the Beast, too, but he doubted if the Count would. 'We can take a chance!' he bellowed above the roar of the diving biplane.

'We ain't got no alternative!' Otto yelled grimly, knocking the last of the broken glass from the shattered windscreen and thrusting his Colt up and on to the frame for support, eyes fixed now on the plane.

'*Here she comes!*' the Beast cried and ducked.

Twin spurts of angry scarlet flame came from right and left of the whirling engine. Red tracer zipped through the air. Friar Tuck watched fascinated as it struck up little spurts of dust on the road to their front, hurrying with ever-increasing speed towards the car. He hit the brakes. The car shuddered to a stop, nearly sending Otto over the bonnet. He caught himself just in time as the plane howled over their heads and the tracer missed so closely that he could feel its glowing heat on his cheeks as it swept by. 'Good thinking, Friar Tuck!' he yelled, as the car charged forward once more. 'But for Chrissake, tell me next time. I nearly went—'

He broke off. Behind him the Beast had recovered his nerve and was beginning to snap off single aimed shots from his Italian pistol as the biplane came round in a tight turn and now attempted to shoot up the car from the rear.

Friar Tuck, his face glistening with sweat, bent low over the wheel and clamped his foot down hard on the accelerator. The road whizzed by. The engine snarled. The car shook violently, as if it might fall apart at any moment under that impossible strain. Otto flashed a look behind him. The racing wheels were kicking up a tremendous cloud of white dust through which he could barely make out the biplane's dim shape. 'Come on, Friar! Come on! We're nearly there!'

'I'm doing my frigging best!' Friar Tuck yelled above the ear-splitting roar of the biplane's radial engine as it came diving in for the kill.

Now the entrance to the steel bridge was perhaps some hundred metres away. But the biplane was almost on top of them. Again its machine-guns started to chatter. Angry flame stabbed the dust cloud. The Count howled suddenly as he was struck a red-hot blow on his arm. He flashed a look down to see his sleeve was red with blood. His face paled. 'God in heaven!' he cried, amazed at the fact that this could happen to *him* – in his years of self-dramatization and histrionics he had never believed that *he* could be hurt, 'I've been hit!'

No one took any notice and he slumped back into his seat moaning softly, composing his features nobly (as he told himself) for the inevitable end, as the car and the plane raced for the bridge.

Again Friar Tuck hit the brakes. The car shuddered to a stop, shimmying all over the road for one long frightening instant, seemingly determined to overturn. Then as the stench of burnt rubber assailed their nostrils, Friar Tuck slammed home first gear and with sweat dropping from his eyebrows like grey pearls, swung her round and into the entrance of the bridge.

'*Good!*' Otto whooped triumphantly and resisted a temptation to slap Friar Tuck across the back just in time, '*We've done it! Let the shitting fly-boy try to hit us here!*' He relaxed a little as the car started to bump over the rough plank road, their flanks now protected by the stout steel girders which rose to a height of four metres on either side.

It seemed too as if the Italian pilot had realized just how difficult it would now be to attempt to shoot up the car, for the biplane had turned in a lazy curve and as the pilot throttled back almost to stalling speed, it hovered above the river observing their slow progress across the bridge.

'You can figure out what he's gonna do, can't you, Otto?' Friar Tuck said, freeing one hand to wipe the sweat from his glistening crimson face, savouring these few moments of relative safety.

'What?'

'The spaghetti shit is gonna wait for us to come out of the other end. We'll have to take that curve in second, *dead slow*, and then he's down gunning for us.'

'But why not go straight on – surprise him – and head straight for the wood?'

'No can do,' Friar Tuck answered without fear in his voice, as the exit from the bridge started to loom up ever closer and the danger commenced once more, 'that vegetation looks too lush to me. My guess is that it's rice paddy. We would go right up to the axle in the mud and then we really would be sitting ducks.'

'What are you going to do then, Friar?' Otto asked, as the American changed down to second once more and prepared to take the steep bend at the exit.

'That sure is the sixty-four dollar question, Otto. But never fear, my friend, I'm thinking on it.'

Surprisingly enough, however, it was not the American but the Count who came up with the answer to that fateful question as they prepared to take the bend. He had now recovered a little from the shock of his shoulder wound and said, 'We must do the unexpected, Friar.'

'How do you mean, Count?'

'From up there he can see the state of the vegetation too. I am sure he has recognized that that is rice paddy and that we won't be able to drive the car through it, so what will he anticipate?'

'That we'll stay on the road, Count,' Otto snapped, impatient as always with the older man who was inclined to be long-winded at such moments when he was the centre of attraction. 'For shit's sake, get on with it!'

The Count said soothingly, 'Patience, Otto, my dear boy, I am getting on with it. Let us go straight into the rice paddy. He'll overshoot and by the time he has recovered we'll be in the wood and safe – at least for the time being.'

The Friar sucked his teeth, face glum. 'I don't know, Count. I haven't a clue just how deep a rice paddy is. For all I know we could be up to our necks in water and mud and that would make fast movement impossible.'

'Piss or get off the pot!' Otto snapped crudely, as the corner loomed every closer.

'All right, we'll do it,' the big American snorted, mind made up. 'But don't blame me if you all end up with a hole in yer head.' He gripped the wheel more firmly as the biplane came zooming in at tree-top level in a low dive. 'Hold tight, *here we go!*'

Gears snarled as the big tourer hit the bend. To their left the white road went off at a right angle. To their front was the embankment with beyond and below at a depth of a metre the shimmering wet green orderly rows of the rice paddy, stretching a hundred metres or more to the shelter of the thick pines beyond. The bumper scraped against one of the stone markers. Slugs howled off the road to their left. Ricochets whined off the steel girders. The car lurched suddenly. There was the sickening sound of metal rending and abruptly the air was full of the cloying stench of escaping gasoline. 'Gas tank gone!' Friar Tuck yelled as the speedometer needle swung wildly to the left.

The Beast yelled with alarm as the tourer's bonnet sank and he lost his hold. Next instant he was flying over it to disappear into a fountain of muddy water. The engine stalled and suddenly the tourer was sinking. Frantically the other three scrambled over the side to drop waist-deep in the paddy, just as the Beast came up spluttering, his face covered with mud and greenery.

Otto pulled him upright. 'Get that shit off your face,' he cried above the roar of the biplane's engine, as the angry frustrated pilot who had been caught by surprise by the unexpected manoeuvre pulled the plane round in a steep tight curve and prepared to come in again. 'Run for it!'

Now the four began to plough madly through the paddy-field. The mud below seemed to suck at their feet, clinging to them with grasping fingers, as if Nature itself wished to see them die. But gasping with the effort, wide, frantic eyes staring at the trees, which were their salvation, they struggled desperately on.

'*Duck!*' Friar Tuck yelled desperately, and flung himself into the paddy in a shallow dive as the biplane came howling in at tree-top height, machine-guns hammering away savagely.

Little angry spurts of brown water erupted all around them as the tracer cut the air about their crouched soaked bodies. An ear-splitting moment of absolute terror and then they were all up again plodding forward, feeling the water getting deeper as they approached the centre of the paddy-field and their progress slowing down accordingly.

Otto flashed a wild look to his right. The bastard was going to come in again. In a tight curve, brown smoke trailing from its engine, the biplane swung in for another attack. Suddenly Otto was overcome by a mad unreasoning rage. He stopped where he stood, water up to his waist, while the others waded on furiously, desperately attempting to get to the cover of the trees before it was too late.

The plane came ever closer. He could see its every detail quite clearly now as it came in from the sun, stark black against the bright burning yellow of the sky. Like some latter-day David he raised his pistol. The plane was less than a hundred metres away now. Instinctively Otto knew the unknown Italian pilot – a white blur behind the racing blades of the propellor – had taken up the challenge. He was concentrating on that lone figure standing up to his waist in the paddy. Slowly, carefully, Otto began to take aim.

The noise of the engine was deafening. Still Otto did not waver. The sun vanished. Now the plane dominated his whole world. Angry little red lights started to crackle the length of its wings. Otto took first pressure. He was completely calm and unafraid. Tracer erupted all around him. He could hear it hiss and cut the air, feeling the warmth of the bullets on his skinny body. He did not move. It was as if the blood in his veins had turned to ice; he had never felt more sure of himself in all his twenty-four years of existence. Second pressure. The racket was ear-splitting now. It seemed that nothing could stop the plane smashing right into this puny figure poised in the middle of the lush-green field. At the very last moment, Otto fired.

The slug smacked right into the gleaming perspex of the cockpit. It disappeared in a sudden bright spider's web. Otto caught one last glimpse of the pilot's terrified face, distorted a thousand times by that cracked surface, hands raised in fear and supplication in front of him. Next instant he ducked below the surface of the water, as the biplane screamed in on its final dive.

Its left wing hit the paddy, dragging a trail of water behind it. Somehow it righted itself. But only momentarily. With frightening abruptness its nose dipped and went straight into the ground. There was a thunderous explosion. Dramatically the plane disintegrated, showering the paddy-field with bits and pieces of metal and equipment. Slowly a mushroom of black smoke started to ascend into the still yellow air. Wearily Otto began to plough forward to where the others waited for him, mud-soaked and awed, in the cover of the trees. They had done it.

One hour later they found the Hermann Goering Division. There was no mistaking the heavy solid tramp of German infantry and that harsh masculine song, as the long column of bronzed young men, their blond cropped heads bared to the midday sun, came stamping up the road, their faces set, keen and confident like the veterans they were . . .

PART TWO: THE SICILY CAPER

'My favourite general is George S. Patton Junior. Some of our generals, such as Stilwell, have developed a sly ability to simulate human beings. But Patton always behaves as a general should. His side arms are as clean as his tongue is foul. And the special uniforms, which he designs himself, are calculated, as were the ox horns of the ancient Gothic chieftains, to strike terror in the hearts of the enemy.

Dwight Macdonald, 1944

ONE

General Baron Benno von Borkenheim sat up on the old cavalry saddle which served him as a seat and stared hard out of the window at the strange little procession which was making its way down the cypress-lined gravel drive which led up to his Headquarters.

In front came a couple of his panzer grenadiers, their bayonets fixed. Behind them was a large chubby fellow dressed as a monk who looked definitely out of place, and next to him an evil looking individual, dressed entirely in black: both of them had their hands clasped on their heads in the fashion of prisoners. To their rear came a tall blond chap with a tough handsome face and bright blue winning eyes, and at his side was an older man carrying a pistol, whose every gesture seemed flamboyant and theatrical, and whose handsome face was definitely familiar.

Von Borkenheim sat even more erect, the metal located at various spots in his skinny mutilated body squeaking audibly as he did so. 'I say, von Soest,' he exclaimed to his monocled aide, 'I do believe . . . Of course, it is! That chap waving that popgun around so damned carelessly – is old Werner von der Weide. Of the *Abwehr*,' he added, as if that explained everything. 'But what in three devils' name is he doing here?' General von Borkenheim swung his wooden leg over the saddle easily. 'Come on, young fellow-me-lad, let's see what that old rogue has been up to now!'

The panzer grenadiers clicked rigidly to attention as the slim immaculate figure, followed by his staff officers, emerged from the door of his villa HQ; and Otto halted at the rear of the little column had an opportunity to take in the General's appearance. The Count had been right, the General was indeed a connoisseur of collecting wounds. Quite a lot of him seemed to be missing as, creaking audibly, cap set at a rakish angle over his eye-patch, empty left sleeve tucked neatly into his gleaming leather belt, he limped up to the waiting men.

Count von der Weide lowered his pistol and chortled happily, 'Benno, old house!'

'Werner, you rogue!' the General exclaimed and the two of them fell into each other's arms happily slapping one another on the back, as if they were choking and needed the air. Then the General released himself and looked with professional interest at the Count's roughly bandaged wounded arm. 'Just a scratch,' he declared after a moment. 'Can't have the divisional surgeon take off your flipper for that, Werner. But then,' he added with a shrug of his thin shoulders, 'you aren't a soldier, are you. Don't need the trappings of the trade, do you? Now then, what have we here?' For the first time he looked at Otto and the two Americans.

'Benno,' the Count declared, putting away the pistol and clicking to attention, falling into his new role one hundred per cent as always, 'I bring you a battle.'

'A battle, Werner?' the General echoed and all around him there was a hushed intake of breath from the surrounding staff officers, as if something of great and lasting significance had been expressed.

The Count beamed at his old friend, obviously happy that he had been able to bring him such good news. 'Yes, a great battle.'

General von Borkenheim's one eye gleamed excitedly and Otto noticed that his one remaining hand had begun to tremble violently, as if he were having the greatest of difficulty in controlling his tension. 'Against whom, Werner? Against whom?'

The Count paused, savouring this moment, knowing all

eyes were fixed on him, 'The Englishman, Benno. The Englishman, General Montgomery!' he declared.

Beside himself with joy General von Borkenheim stamped his good foot down hard on the gravel. 'By God, Werner, that indeed is good news! Last couple of years we've fought nothing but a bunch of greasy spaghetti-eaters and lousy Russkis. Be good again to fight against the Tommies. They are at least from one's own social class, gentlemen. Now come on,' he thrust his arm through that of his old friend, 'let's get inside. You must tell me more.'

Numbly, Otto, wondering as always at the manner in which the military, whatever their nationality, took to the bloody business of slaughtering their fellow soldiers, trailed behind . . .

High above the villa in the burning hot foothills, Colonel Blackie Burrows lowered his glasses momentarily, hawked in the fashion of a North West Frontier tribesman, and spat angrily on the hot rock behind which he and Carruthers were hiding. 'Well, there we have it, don't we, young Carruthers,' he barked, focusing his glasses on the villa once again.

'What sir?' Carruthers asked, as bewildered as ever as he watched the little procession below disappear into the gleaming white villa.

Carruthers was dressed in what the Intelligence quartermaster had thought was typical Italian gear: a felt hat complete with long drooping pheasant feather, a short sleeveless jacket adorned with brass buttons, knee breeches, woollen stockings and heavy brogues. Looking at himself in the mirror back in Algiers, he had exclaimed in dismay, 'Oh my God, Q, all I need now is a monkey on my shoulder and my hurdi-gurdi, and you'd take me for a frigging Eyetie organ-grinder!' Irony had been wasted on the quartermaster. 'I like to be a trend-setter, Carruthers,' he had said proudly.

'More like a bloody Irish Setter!' he had sneered, but his words had had no effect. It was therefore dressed as an 'Eyetie organ-grinder' that he had parachuted into Sicily two days before. Now he and his chief observed the villa which they knew to be the headquarters of the Hermann Goering Panzer Division.

'Worse than anything I've ever seen in twenty-five years in the Great Game,' Colonel Burrows snorted. 'Not even your Johnny Pathan would sink *that* low!'

'I'm afraid I don't follow you at all, sir.'

'Plain as the nose on your face, Carruthers. Those devilish Yanks and the Boche they trained back in Africa – they've obviously gone over to the Hermann Goering. And you can guess what they are going to hand over to the Huns, can't you.'

Carruthers looked at his chief aghast, forgetting in his shock even the fact that Colonel Burrows was the most improbable-looking Italian imaginable. In his check plus fours, striped black-and-white shirt, and black beret set at a rakish angle on his cropped white head, he looked like a cross between a French onion-seller and a shabby Scots golfer down on his luck. Even the limp rose that he had perched behind his right ear – 'wops always carry roses behind their ears, never think of anything but fornicating' – added nothing to his Italian disguise. 'Sir, you don't think they'd tell the enemy *that*, do you?'

'I certainly do, Carruthers. Look!'

Carruthers stared down at the villa through his binoculars. A white-coated orderly was hurrying into the villa, bottle and glasses balanced on a gleaming tray held up high.

'They normally don't serve bubbly to POWs do they?' Burrows barked harshly. 'What?'

Numbly Carruthers nodded his head in agreement, telling himself again that this Intelligence business which he had entered so recently was funny, very funny indeed; most of the time, a chap's right hand didn't know what his left was doing.

'But by God, they'll pay for it!' Burrows said angrily, lowering his glasses and catching his rose just in time, as it tumbled from his ear.

'How do you mean, sir?' Carruthers asked, following suit and unpleasantly aware of his thick rough shirt sticking to his sweaty back.

Burrows looked at him hard. 'Carruthers, we can't allow them to get away with it, even if it costs our lives. We can't let Monty down, what?' He fumbled for his pistol and then satisfied that it was safely tied to his leg and dangling down the front of his voluminous plus fours by string, added, '*Tonight!*'

'Tonight, sir?' Carruthers asked, thinking that any casual observer at this moment might have thought his chief was gratifying an urgent sexual need.

'Yes, we go in after 'em.' His bright little gimlet-like eyes gleamed hard. 'Cold steel, I think.'

'Yes sir, cold steel it is,' Carruthers echoed in a sinking little voice . . .

Inside the big cool room, still heavy with the odour of garlic and green peppers that its former Italian owners had left behind, the General rocked excitedly back and forth on his saddle and barked, 'Of course, Werner, we've been expecting the enemy to have a crack at us ever since Rommel made a balls-up of things in North Africa. Never did think much of that chap. I believe his father was an elementary school teacher or something petite bourgeois of that kind. Not at all our class of officer. That's why the High Command ordered the Division to this arse-hole of a place, so that the Hermann Goering could be switched to either the beaches around Gela, or those at Cassibile in the Gulf of Noto.' He beamed at his old friend, who had just explained what had brought him and his 'two prisoners' to Hermann Goering HQ. 'Naturally I didn't think then that the move would give me a chance to have a crack at their Montgomery chap.' His one eye gleamed excitedly at the prospect. 'Imagine pushing him back into the sea on the first day of his attack! The first time the Tommies attack Continental Europe in force since 1940 and it ends in another Dunkirk, though the Tommies seem to like that sort of thing,' he conceded. 'Strange people. They tell me they eat kidneys and fried fish for breakfast. No matter. It would be a great victory. Undoubtedly the Führer would create a special decoration for me, especially if by chance I was wounded leading my brave fellows into the attack.' He glanced down at his spare mutilated frame, hung with gleaming enamel decorations and bright medal ribbons, as if looking for a suitable portion of it which might be still spared. 'That Rommel chap would certainly have a blue fit then.'

Otto standing moodily at the window, sipping ice-cold *spumanti*, and watching Friar Tuck and the Beast being led away to the HQ's little jail located between the other ranks' latrines and the officers' brothel, sighed heavily – the world he had inhabited since 1939 was crazy. All these upper and middle class folks seemed to have their heads in their arses, born without common-sense, taken up by any and each mad idea that came floating their way, posing and posturing all the time, as if life was one big shitting game. '*But ain't it, Otto?*' that insidious little voice that always functioned somewhere in the further recesses of his brain at such moments asked cunningly in the working-class accents of his native Berlin. '*One big lark from beginning to end until you're finally looking up at the taties from two metres of earth, Otto, old mate?*'

Otto took a deep sip of his cheap Italian champagne, wished it had been a good solid tonsil-shocking schnapps, dismissed the insidious voice and concentrated on the conversation between the General and his old friend.

'The prisoners, those American chappies,' Benno von Borkenheim was saying, moving back and forth on his saddle excitedly, 'they gave no clue to when the Tommies will be coming, Werner?'

The Count shook his head and Otto was relieved that he was sensible enough to remember that he should not reveal the date of the landing. The silly bastards were going to knock shit out of each other sooner or later, but still he did not want the Tommies to walk straight into a trap once they started leaving their landing-barges. The poor buck-teethed bastards had enough problems as it was already. 'No, I've tried everything with them, Benno, short of downright torture—'

Benno von Borkenheim sucked in his breath severely. 'Can't have that sort of thing, Werner, can we? Leave that nasty business to those working class chaps of the Gestapo. I always think Intelligence is a much too dirty business to leave to anyone but gentlemen. No matter, we know enough. We know roughly where this Montgomery fellow is going to land and we know his style.' He winked knowingly at von der Weide, 'It's a dead give away. The usual long-winded build up to the attack – artillery bombardment, aerial attack, the usual sort of thing. As that poet chappie Heine once remarked when asked where he wanted to be on the Day of Judgment, "England". Asked why, he said, "Because everything happens a hundred years later in that country." Ha, ha, a joke! So, my dear Werner, when Montgomery finally does land my division will be waiting for him.'

The Count smiled nervously. 'Of course it will be Benno. You've always been known as a general who marches to the sound of the guns.'

'Exactly,' Benno agreed, cocking his wooden leg over the saddle with a squeak of leather and metal, eye gleaming excitedly. 'We march at dawn! When Montgomery does decide to come, *we'll drive him back into the sea!*'

But Baron von Borkenheim was not fated to achieve that aim, for already nemesis in the unlucky shapes of Colonel Burrows and Captain Carruthers were on their way . . .

TWO

'Keep the sun behind you, Carruthers. That way you can control your own shadow, just the way the wily Pathan does and merge it with the others,' Colonel Blackie Burrows hissed. 'Watch for fruit trees. Usually full of bloody birds. Make a terrible racket if you disturb them. If we bump into cattle which haven't been milked, they'll lick your face and moo. Only thing to do is to lie on your back and milk the things. Got it?'

'Got it, sir,' Carruthers replied dutifully, refraining from reminding the old man that it was almost dark, there weren't any fruit trees within miles, and he hadn't seen a bloody cow ever since they had dropped into the bloody island.

'Good.' Blackie Burrows surveyed their front severely, eyes narrowed to slits.

To their front the dusk was beginning to shine with a deceptive incandescence, as if everything had been sprinkled with powdered lime. A light wind had sprung up, bringing with it a heavy drift of perfumed grasses and shrubs, bearing an occasional noise from the blacked out villa below, though a clump of pampas grass next to their hiding place sent up a continuous whispering which made it difficult to identify sounds exactly.

Suddenly Blackie saw what he was looking for. A shadow had detached itself from the deeper shadows cast by the wall to the rear of the villa. He reached out and pressed Carruthers' arm hard. '*Sentry!*' he mouthed the word with hardly a sound. 'Got to nobble him first. Got it?'

Carruthers suddenly found it difficult to speak; his

mouth seemed to have dried up. Finally he managed to croak, 'Yes, sir.'

'All right, laddie,' Carruthers gulped again as Blackie Burrows pulled something from inside his plus fours by means of the hole he had made in the pocket. It gleamed a dull silver in the velvet dusk of the Mediterranean night. 'Cold steel, as I said, Carruthers. Come on!'

With surprising alacrity for such an old man, he rose to his feet and with a reluctant Carruthers trailing behind began to advance stealthily on the white-painted villa.

Minutes passed. Carruthers' nerves jingled like electric wires, his every sense primed by danger, his attention so strained to catch the slightest sound, the slightest movement, that every moment was like a drop of burning hot liquid added to a bowl that was already brim-full.

Blackie halted so abruptly that Carruthers almost bumped into him. 'There he is!' he hissed. 'Look, he's smoking a filthy weed while on sentry. Ought to bang him on a charge for that kind of behaviour. What?'

'Sir,' Carruthers echoed, taking in the faint red glow of a lit cigarette some twenty or so yards away and wondering that the old man could be concerned about the slackness of the German Army at this particular, very frightening moment. 'What do we do?'

Blackie chuckled softly. It wasn't a pleasant sound. '*You* do nothing, young fellow-me-laddie. Got to leave this one to an old North West Frontier hand. Ape Johnny Pathan you know. I'll hoot like an owl when I'm finished. Then you come running. And watch out for unmilked cows!'

Carruthers would have groaned out loud, if he had had the strength to do so.

Blackie hushed forward. Now he could make out the sentry quite clearly as he stood there in the doorway, cigarette protected from any nosey superior in a cupped hand, his chin lit a faint red by its glow. He smiled grimly to himself. The fool had his rifle slung. By the time he pulled it off his shoulder, he would be dead.

He advanced on tiptoe, knife held firmly against his right hip, as he had seen the frontiersmen do it. Now he was only a couple of yards away from the unsuspecting German. He knew he couldn't conceal his approach any longer. In spite of the faint noises he could hear coming from the main building, the German would hear him at any moment. He drew a deep breath and told himself he was perfectly calm, which was quite true; Blackie Burrows had never experienced a moment's doubt or fear in his whole life. He dived forward, knife at the ready . . .

Otto sat on a ration box in the makeshift cell, facing a weary Friar Tuck and the Beast, whose supper he had just brought in and watched them eat the stale salami sandwich and wash it down with thin sour local red wine. 'Compliments of the Count,' he had explained, handing them over the wicker-covered fat bottle. 'He shouldn't have bothered,' Friar Tuck had exclaimed wry-faced, after the first pull at its contents. Now for the first time since they had started on their impossible mission to Sicily, the two Americans were obviously worried, Otto could see that all right. And he knew why. Both of them had suddenly realized the enormity of their betrayal and its consequences for them. The thought gave him mild pleasure. For the first time that overweening, unthinking American confidence of theirs seemed undermined. He broke his silence to rub salt in the wound. 'Have you gents ever thought what will happen to you personally if the Baron and his panzers give Montgomery a real hard knock on the beaches tomorrow?'

'Tomorrow!' Friar Tuck gasped, salami suddenly halted at his mouth. 'Is tomorrow the tenth?'

Otto nodded.

'What do you mean, Otto?' the Beast asked. 'We're under the Count's protection aren't we? What's there to beef about?'

Otto took his time, restraining his natural impulse to tell

the tall skinny saturnine American exactly what he thought about Count von der Weide's protection. 'This. If the Tommies get a bloody nose and do a bunk, what's going to happen to you two?'

'Happen to us?' Friar Tuck scratched his big tonsured skull. 'Jeez, I never thought about that.'

'Exactly.'

'Don't be so darned high and mighty, Otto,' the Beast said angrily. 'What will happen to us?'

Otto shrugged. 'If you're lucky, it'll be a POW camp for you. If you're unlucky,' he didn't finish his sentence. Instead he clicked his right forefinger back and forth, as if he were pulling a trigger.

Friar Tuck went pale beneath his suntan. The Beast said, 'But the Krauts wouldn't do *that*, Otto! After all, as far as this Baron von Borkenheim guy knows, we're the guys who passed the Count his information about Montgomery's landings in the first place.'

'Tell that to the Gestapo,' Otto answered, enjoying the look of fear that was beginning to creep across the sadist's face. For once Captain I. Wipem was getting a taste of what he would undoubtedly call 'his own medicine'.

'What do *you* think we should do, Otto?' Friar Tuck asked, his sausage sandwich forgotten now.

Otto looked carefully to left and right, as if someone might be listening; it was that old habit he had brought with him from Germany and had not been able to shake off, although it was two years now since he had seen his native country. 'A bunk, that's what I think we should do. At the first available opportunity. Whatever those meatheads of generals do, Mrs Stahl's handsome son thinks, it's better to let them get on with it – *without us!*'

'You mean make a break for it?' the Beast asked stupidly.

'Yes,' Otto sneered contemptuously. 'Or should I draw yer a picture? Once I get the Count out of the clutches of that walking skeleton, I say we should be off. Right smartish!'

Friar Tuck nodded his agreement, and the Beast,

obviously warming to the idea now, asked, 'But where is the Count, Otto?'

Otto forced a grin, though at that particular moment with a dangerous and uncertain future looming up in front of him, he didn't particularly feel like grinning. 'Where? A place where I'd like to be at this moment. But I'm classed as another rank and other ranks in the German Army on active duty are supposed to look after their desires in the thunderboxes dallying with the one-handed widow.'

'What in Christ's name are you talking about, Otto?' the Beast snapped. 'Talk American!'

Otto was not offended. 'The *Herr Baron*, you will be pleased to know,' he explained, 'has invited his old comrade-in-arms *Graf* von der Weide into the officers' *puff* after dinner. A sort of going-away present, you might say, before the battle commences.'

'What's a *puff*, Otto?' Friar Tuck asked.

By way of an answer, Otto jerked his thumb to the cell wall to the left. 'The HQ's latrines, Friar.' His thumb jerked to the right, 'The *puff*, the officers' brothel to you.' He grinned maliciously. 'At this particular moment, gents, you might say you're between *shit* and *sex*! If the Count's lucky this evening, he's gonna get sex. And if you two are unlucky, you're gonna get—'

'Say no more, Otto, say no more!' Friar Tuck interrupted him abruptly. 'I read you all too well. You've got to get us out of here tonight!'

The sentry lay on his back dead. An arm and a leg were sprawled out and the other pair were tucked under his body in an odd, unnatural way. Blood flooded the front of his ripped tunic. Carruthers gulped hard, feeling as if he had swallowed a football. 'What now, sir?' he hissed.

Calmly Blackie Burrows wiped the blade of his knife clean on the dead man's tunic and said, 'First we kill the senior German officers down to the rank of full colonel, then we deal with those deuced traitors,' he said firmly, straightening up.

Carruthers looked at the old man, as if he had just gone mad.

'*Generals . . . down* to . . . *full colonels?*' he stammered.

Blackie Burrows beamed at him in the darkness. 'Good chap. You've got it. Come on!'

They sped silently along the cypress-lined path which flanked the rear of the villa. Suddenly a door opened to their front. A yellow knife of light slid into the glowing velvet darkness. They halted as one. Carruthers' blood froze. He could hear his heart pounding so loudly that he thought the man standing there puffing away at a cigar must hear it. But he didn't. Instead he took a last draw at his cigar, dropped and crushed it audibly under his heel in the gravel before returning to the house and closing the door behind him.

Blackie Burrows sniffed the air like a blood-hound scenting its prey before announcing, 'Expensive cigar. Only senior chaps smoke weed like that. Come on, Carruthers. We're on to them!' There was no mistaking the excitement in the old boy's voice now. Miserably Carruthers stole after him.

Cautiously, very cautiously, Blackie Burrows opened the back door, while Carruthers crouched there, knees bent, eyes bulging, pistol clasped in a sweat-wet hand like one of those cowboys in the big-shoot-out in a Hollywood western whose fate it was to be shot first.

The corridor which was revealed was empty, but now for the first time he became aware of a strange rhythmic squeaking, which began to gather perceptibly in speed, as it slowly began to dawn on the two Englishmen crouching there what it was. 'I say, Carruthers,' Blackie Burrows identified the sound finally in a shocked voice, 'I do believe, no I'm sure – *somebody is fornicating up there . . . !*'

*

'My dear Werner,' the Baron said expansively, dipping the butt of his cigar in cognac and smiling pleasantly at the whores grouped at the far end of the company waiting for the two old comrades to make their final choice, 'I have, as you know, three special talents.' He looked down modestly at his one hand and its well-manicured, lacquered nails, 'fighting, fearlessness and – er – *fornication*.' He chuckled at his own humour. 'I always say, that a chap who won't fornicate won't fight, what.'

'I suppose, Benno,' the Count said a little unhappily, eyeing the females, who the Baron called *poules de luxe*, though to his untutored gaze they looked a very unluxurious bunch of females.

'Yes,' the Baron said expansively, pointing his cigar at the waiting women like a deadly weapon. 'A good gallop with a willing wench before battle, gets a chap's blood roused, I maintain. Now then, Werner, we haven't got all night. To *nos moutons*, which one are *you* going to have? They're all certified by the divisional sawbones as being fit for human consumption. Ha, ha! Free from pox and sundry other disorders of the female breed.'

The Count looked across at the waiting women, all in various stages of undress, smiling madly with the fake concupiscence of the professional wanton. 'I don't quite know, Benno,' he replied uneasily.

'The choice is good and I can recommend all of 'em. I have had the lot of course. There isn't much of a turn-round in these remote places.' He pointed his cigar at a hard-faced ageing Italian blonde, her fat body forced into a tight black satin corset, which attempted to hold up her sagging breasts and failed lamentably, her plump legs encased in high, laced boots. 'That's Sophia,' he said. 'They say she can bring a mummy back to life. I remember when old Field Marshal—' he stopped suddenly, cocking his head to one side. 'Did you hear that, sounded like a plane?'

The Count, glad of the interruption, cocked his head and listened too. But all he could hear was the rusty squeaking of bedsprings coming from the floor above. He shook his head.

The Baron dismissed the noise. 'Must have been my imagination. Now back to the fillies.' He chuckled delightedly. 'I fancy Renate over there myself. She knows a few tricks that bring a sparkle to an old man's eye, I can tell you, Werner.' He leaned forward and whispered excitedly into the other man's ear.

The Count's face flushed an embarrassed red. 'Oh, I say, Benno, she doesn't do that, does she?' he exclaimed.

'But yes, my dear fellow – and with a broomstick too. Yes, that girl really knows how to make a chap's heart beat a little faster.' He licked his lips in anticipation, his false teeth gleaming in the sparkling light of the candles. 'Unless of course, you wish for—' The Baron never finished his offer, for at that very moment, the quadruple flak cannon located outside the villa burst into frenetic life and there was the sudden whine of a stricken aircraft coming down in its last dive. The room rocked. Glasses started rolling down from the table. The girls screamed. The Count and the Baron sprang to their feet as outside the alarm sirens started to shrill their warning and the tranquillity of the headquarters was broken by the blast of NCOs' whistles and the rush of heavy feet as men pelted to their posts.

A tremendous crash, which set the villa shaking back and forth, as if hit by a hurricane. Next instant a great hole appeared in the roof. In a cloud of plaster, snapped lathes and broken tiles, a khaki-clad figure suspended by what appeared to be a parachute came hurtling into the room, so surprising the Baron that his false teeth fell out of his gaping mouth and tumbled into his broad cognac glass to rest there leering up at his shaken face.

Crouched in a heap of broken tiles on the floor the British parachutist stared up at the toothless General and breathed in purest cockney, '*Bleedin' hell, what a cock-up! Right into the middle of a Jerry HQ. What a typical ferking Fred Karno's . . .*'

THREE

'*It was a complete military balls up!*' Otto Stahl would recall nearly forty years after the strange events of that night. 'According to the official report, which I read a couple of months after the war was over, compiled by some military genius, English or American, it doesn't matter, they're all the shitting same – *thick from the neck upwards!* – the anti-aircraft fire had considerable volume and produced unfortunate effects on the American pilots who had never seen action before. Their evasive tactics greatly increased the difficulty and hazard of jumping for our first wave of paratroopers, who were leading the invasion of Sicily.'

'*Unfortunate effect*, my sacred arse! The Yanks got the wind up, as soon as the macaroni flak opened up off the coast! They started dropping the Tommy paras and releasing the gliders all over the show so that the Tommies were dropping and coming down over half of Sicily that night. They blanketed the area occupied by the Hermann Goering and the other Eyetie divisions, which in a way was fortunate for us because if it hadn't have been for that balls up, things might not have turned out the way they did, which wasn't particularly good any road.

'That night was mass confusion. I'd never seen anything like it since the day a Tommy bomb had hit the sewage works back in Berlin-Kreuzberg and splattered half of Berlin with wet shit! Tommy paras were coming down all over the show. Some of them didn't even know whether they were in Sicily or Italy, they were so mixed up. Gliders came careening in over the fields snapping off the trees like they were matchsticks and sending the wops running off to church and the holy rollers splashing out the holy water like ready money as if the end of the world was upon 'em.

'The HQ of the HG, natch, was in a complete panic. The staff officers were doing their nut trying to get the Div on the road, while the pavement pounders in the officers' and gentlemen's knocking shop were alternatively having hysterics and sticking their tongues down the Tommy para's throat and yelling he was their "liberator". I wouldn't have been surprised if the poor bugger was tongued to death that night as he lay in the middle of the floor with his ankle broken. But then there are worse ways to go, aren't there?'

'All I knew that night of July 9th, 1943 was that I had to get out of the damned place before the balloon really went up! I'd been around long enough by that time to know that in that kind of confused balls up, people pulled their triggers first and asked the right questions later.'

'Come on!' Otto cried above the snap-and-crack of the wild fire-fight taking place outside, springing into the cell over the body of the sentry he had just knocked unconscious. 'Let's make steam! We've got to get the Count!'

The two Americans needed no urging. Friar Tuck ripped up his skirt and bolted out of the wide-open cell-door, while the Beast followed suit, pausing only to bend down and grab the sentry's pistol.

Outside in the glowing night all was complete confusion. Officers bellowed orders and others counter-orders. Men ran back and forth. Over at the motor pool, drivers frantically attempted to start their motors. Tracer zipped back and forth like flights of angry red hornets. Flares hissed into the sky, green, white, silver, red. Yet another glider, a monstrous black shape, its tow rope loosed far over the sea, came hushing in, to hit the fields beyond in a great shower of stones and dust. Almost instantly dazed men stumbled from it to run blindly into the massed machine-guns of the HQ's defensive platoon dug in around the villa.

Otto ran into the house where an officer, naked save for his boots and a monocle stuck in his left eye, tried to stop him. Otto's fist slammed into his skinny guts. He doubled up, the monocle popping out of his eye with surprise.

'You ought to be had up for indecent exposure!' Otto cried, as he sprang over him and pelted up the stairs, followed by the other two. He flung open the door.

Half-naked women were everywhere, screaming hysterically and tearing at their dyed locks in true Italian fashion. On the floor a grinning Tommy, half buried in tiles, his face covered in lipstick grinned up at them. He seemed to be drunk. 'Bleeding nice turn-up for the books, ain't it,' he chortled happily a propos of nothing. Otto ignored him, as he flashed a wild look around the place.

'Where's the Count—' He stopped short and ducked.

From behind the tattered screen to the rear of the *salon*, a portly officer naked to the waist raised his pistol. The explosion in those close quarters was deafening. Behind him the large mirror which had been an essential part of the fat Sophia's act shattered into a thousand pieces. She screamed with rage, so much so that both her pendulous dugs popped from the tight confines of her black satin corset. '*Beast!*' she cried, besides herself with rage. '*Fornicating German beast!*' With one desperate bound she had launched herself at the surprised officer. They went down in a heap, Sophia on top of him, her long red nails clawing at his plump face. '*Il Conte*,' he demanded, grabbing for his pistol in what he thought was a dramatic masterly manner, '*dove il conte?*'

'Here, Otto, here! Oh thank the Good Lord that you have saved me!'

Otto swung round.

The Count, naked to the waist and holding his trousers up fearfully, stood in the doorway, dominated by a large fat Italian whore. Otto's mouth dropped open with surprise, for the whore, who had a definite suspicion of a moustache above her thick sensual lips, not only wore exceedingly high heeled boots but carried a thin cruel-looking black whip in her hamlike fist. The Beast gasped in admiration and said, 'I say, that's a rather nice piece of leather. Give it a swish, woman!'

'Shut up!' Otto snapped recovering from the sight. 'Get your shirt, Count. Quick! We're off!'

'Anything . . . anything to get away from her.' He shot the big woman a frightened look and, sidling by her swiftly, grabbed his shirt.

Otto wasted no more time. From down below there came the sound of heavy nailed boots clattering up the stairs and he didn't need a fortune-teller to inform him that they meant trouble.

'You.' He grabbed the nearest whore cruelly by the arm. 'Is there a back way out of this place?'

'*Si . . . si, signor!*' the whore quavered, obviously terrified of this no-nonsense German. '*Preggo . . .*'

Hurriedly the four of them followed the whore who, even at this moment of extreme crisis, could not quite abandon the professional wiggle of her plump black-lace covered buttocks. Behind them in the rubble the drunken Tommy paratrooper pushed away the two importuning whores and cried happily, 'Let me know who won the war, cock!' Next moment he was submerged once more in warm plump Italian flesh.

'There!' the whore declared, opening the door to the rear of the *salon*, and screamed shrilly the next moment as a burst of machine-gun fire ripped the length of the wall to the front.

'Out of the way!' Otto yelled. 'Come on – at the double now!'

Crouched low the four of them darted the length of the long room. To their right, the single window was suddenly bright with silver light. 'Searchlight,' Friar Tuck yelled in alarm. '*Watch it!*'

The machine-gun chattered again. Glass splintered. The window disappeared in a gleaming spider's web of broken glass. Plaster rained down upon their bent heads. Ricochets howled off the bullet-pocked walls. Otto felt the heat of a slug on his left cheek as it hissed by and erupted in a tiny spurt of angry blue flame just next to his head. Then they were through the door to the rear of the place.

Otto skidded to a halt. Two strange figures were crouched there in the shrubbery. By the glowing light of the tracer and the searchlight, he could see they were both dressed in civvies, but there was no mistaking the upturned sweep of the thick black cavalry moustache of the one who looked like an Italian organ-grinder. They were English all right.

'Stop where you are, sir!' the older one of the two cried harshly, fumbling inside the front of his voluminous golfing trousers as if he were going to commit an act of gross sexual indecency at any moment.

Otto didn't give him a chance to find whatever he was looking for. His right foot lashed out. The old man shrieked and went reeling back, looking as if someone had just thrown a handful of strawberry jam at his face.

'I say,' Carruthers blurted out angrily. 'You can't do that sort of thing! It isn't crick—' the protest died on his lips, as Friar Tuck punched him hard in the stomach. He gasped harshly and sat down looking very surprised, mouth gaping like a village idiot.

They rushed on, leaving the two Englishmen recovering in the shrubs behind them.

Now they were running down the cypress-lined drive pursued by wild bursts of tracer. Somehow Otto knew the weapon was not aimed at them, for the Tommy paratroopers were raining down from the sky everywhere, clicking the silly little toy frogs as they did so, as if they were a load of infants celebrating the delights of a newly opened Christmas stocking. Another monstrous glider came hushing out of the sky, its tail a blazing torch. It slammed into the ground a hundred metres to their front and upturned, with crazed airborne soldiers ripping and tearing at its canvas sides to get out before they were consumed by the flames. A Fiat car skidded to a stop. *Carabinieri* in their plumed 19th century high hats tumbled from it, weapons blazing as they did so, slaughtering the helpless, panic-stricken Tommies.

Otto saw red. 'Come on!' he screamed above the mad rattle of the Italians' automatics. 'Let's get those dagoes!'

They streamed forward. The driver who had remained in the car grabbed for his pistol. It was the last thing he ever did. Otto beat him to the draw. He slammed down on the wheel, head striking the horn which added its shrill mechanical noise to the curses and screams of the trapped English survivors and the savage rattle of the cops' automatics, as they slaughtered the red berets.

The Beast fired a burst. Three *carabinieri* dropped, arms flailing the air as they did so. Otto's pistol barked again. One of the cops who had attempted to dive for cover behind the abandoned car went reeling backwards, hands clasped to his shattered face, bright red blood seeping through his tightly pressed fingers, moaning dreadfully as he did so. It took the heart out of the rest of the Italians. As one they dropped their guns and raised their hands in surrender, dark faces and black eyes suddenly fearful.

The Beast raised his pistol deliberately, his skinny face animated by the desire to inflict pain. Otto leapt at him, banging his pistol arm down. 'Stop it!' he cried above the screams of the trapped men, who were being slowly consumed by the flames lashing at their upturned glider. 'There's been enough murder and mayhem.' He aimed a savage kick at the nearest cop. '*Avanti . . . subito . . .*' he commanded, propelling him forward towards the glider. 'And the rest of you, too . . . Go on, help the poor sods!'

Happy and relieved to be still alive, the policemen rushed forward to help. Otto watched their progress for a few moments as they struggled to rescue the Tommies, then, satisfied that they'd saved those that they could, he ran back to the car and pulled the dead driver clear of the wheel.

The noise of the horn stopped immediately, which was a relief. But already another and more fearful noise was beginning to impinge on Otto's consciousness – a strange kind of long-drawn-out howl. He flung a look to the horizon to the south. The sky there was a dull red in half a dozen spots as if some great blast furnace had just begun to operate. Instantly Otto knew what it was. It was the start of the great naval bombardment which heralded the main invasion of Sicily. Soon the landings would commence and Otto knew instinctively that they wouldn't last the night if they were caught out in the open in the middle of this confused lethal mess. 'Come on,' he yelled, 'let's get the hell out of here while there's still time!'

Friar Tuck flung himself carelessly behind the wheel, his habit flying and Otto made a mental note that he would have to remind the big brash American to start wearing underpants. It was positively indecent the way he kept waving his wand every time he opened his legs too wide.

But at that moment Lieutenant Al Cheetham of the OSS was too happy to be worried by such minor details. 'Wheels,' he cried delightedly, as he turned the key and the Fiat's motor sprang into sweet vibrating life the very first time. 'Now we really are cooking with gas, guys! All aboard, let's go!' He gunned the engine impatiently, as the other three tumbled into the car. Next instant they were careering down the road at a hundred kilometres an hour, heading straight for that sinister red glow on the horizon . . .

FOUR

That night Sicily went crazy. The news that the Allies were landing on the island after twenty-one years of domination by the Duce, Benito Mussolini spread like wildfire. Time and time again, the progress of Otto's group to the coast and safety was blocked by the excited, flag-waving citizens, now erupting on to the narrow streets and heedless of the blackout regulations, running wild on a mad wrecking spree. Every little community had the universal bronze statue of a helmeted, heavy-jawed *il Duce* and this it seemed was the first target of their rage: first it was pelted with local tomatoes, spat at, urinated upon by the bolder villagers and then finally with a massive heave-ho tugged by rope from its plinth. 'Jeez,' Friar Tuck breathed, as they watched yet another bronzed Mussolini hit the cobbles to the accompaniment of a wild burst of cheering and the triumphant fanfare of the local voluntary fire-brigade, 'it's like the night the Navy took San Diego apart in 1942!'

Otto had no idea what the night the 'Navy took San Diego apart' was like, indeed didn't even know where San Diego was; all he knew was that he didn't want to waste time in this damned place. By dawn when the dive-bombers would start to come in and no doubt in typical American fashion knocking anybody and anything which stood in the way of the invading troops, he wanted to have his personal head down deep beneath a couple of metres of solid cover. 'Forget 1942, Friar!' he yelled above the frenzied screams and catcalls of the excited Latin mob as they began to indulge themselves in an orgy of destruction, the road now scattered with fascist party books, badges and bits and pieces of black militia uniform, 'let's haul arse out of this place right quick!'

But it was the same in the next village they encountered on their flight to the sea – and the next.

Just before dawn, with the sky towards the east already flushing that dramatic pink that always heralded daybreak along the Mediterranean, they were held up again by a procession of boys of the fascist *balilla* youth movement, marching solemnly towards the town square where the 'sons of the wolf', as they had once proudly called themselves in better days, ceremonially laid down their wooden rifles and pulled off their badges and insignia.

As was usual on such occasions, the Count, now recovered from his encounter with the sadistic whore, was impressed. 'Ah, what brave little fellows,' he enthused, 'how well they are taking it!' Carried away by the enthusiasm of the watching doting crowd, he, too, began to clap as yet another youngster placed his rifle gently on the pile of painted wood and turned manfully away, trying to repress a sad tear.

Otto shook his head in mock wonder. 'Sometimes I wonder, Count, I honestly do, where you've got your head. In your arse—' The words died on his lips, for at the far end of the straight cobbled road which led through the place, the first tank began to edge its way cautiously into the village and a hoarse German voice cried out, '*Mano in alto!*' '*At the double, you macaroni-eaters, get them paws up in the air!*'

Otto's heart sank. He knew instinctively to what outfit those tanks belonged. *The Hermann Goering Division!* Baron von Borkenheim had caught up with the fugitives – *and his tanks were heading for the beach where Patton was going to land!* They had failed. Now they were caught between the devil and the deep blue sea.

With the last of his rapidly vanishing strength of purpose, he croaked, 'Friar you'd better get us out of here damned smartish, or else it's a quick ta-ta to the nearest wall for us, and I don't think his nibs von Borkenheim would be too happy if his firing squad missed!'

Followed by an angry burst of machine-gun fire which scattered the Italian crowd and cooled their ardour for that night, they fled . . .

The mass confusion of that July night, with enemy paratroopers landing along the whole length of his front for no apparent tactical reason and the spontaneous rising of the Sicilians against their fascist masters, blocking the village and town roads everywhere, forced General von Borkenheim's Hermann Goering Panzer Division to swing to the south-west instead of the south-east where Montgomery's Eighth Army was preparing to land. The information made the mutilated Divisional Commander angry; he was going to be cheated of his chance to throw the Englishman who had beaten Rommel into the sea. But he was realistic enough to know that there was nothing he could do about it. He decided to hit the Americans. That dawn as his lead tanks chased Otto's car out of the Sicilian township, with the thunder of the Allied naval bombardment getting ever louder and the whole horizon black with the smoke of exploding shells, he gathered his staff around him and pointed to what would soon be the new front. '*Meine Herren*, out there are the Amis. For the moment as befits a great industrial nation, they are relying on their technical superiority – their planes, their ships, their great naval guns. But soon, they must produce men, men who are prepared to fight and die.' He peered around at his staff with his one eye, 'The question is – are they prepared to do that?' He answered his own question. 'I don't think so. Our plan is simple therefore, gentlemen.' His voice rose harshly, 'we shall drive into their infantry as soon as it lands – full tilt. No mercy will be shown. The first hours will be crucial. We must be ruthless, completely ruthless with ourselves and the enemy.' He drew himself up to his full height. 'By this night we must have thrown the Americans back into the sea. *Meine Herren*, to your commands! I shall lead the first wave personally!' He forced a brief smile. 'Good hunting, gentlemen!' he barked and then they were all running to the waiting tanks. The Herman Goering attack had commenced . . .

By mid-morning that tenth of July 1943, the American bridgehead around Gela was under full attack. Everywhere the positions of the Big Red One, the US Army's premier infantry division, were being pressed devilishly hard by von Borkenheim's panzers so that its commander General Allen, unshaven, red-eyed and very worried, had to order every available divisional gun upfront to help his stalled infantry, rolling them frantically into position to meet the Herman Goering tanks at point-blank range.

By midday, forty of von Borkenheim's tanks had broken through the first infantry positions and were reported heading down the road towards Gela, where the narrow beachhead bulged with the massive heaps of supplies being brought ashore at top speed from the seven hundred small craft which plied back and forth from the fleet to the beach. Another twenty of them had been reported on the other flank of the Big Red One. If these two columns managed to converge at Gela, they would be able to break through the beach. If they succeeded in doing that, not only would the Big Red One be cut off, but the whole beachhead would be endangered and the success of the great invasion.

General Allen ordered every available truck in the division to return to the beach, pick up a cannon and race it back to the front. Desperately he radioed for naval artillery support as the first German tanks started to crawl ever closer to his command post like evil metal predators, their long overhanging cannon swinging from left to right as they sought out their prey.

Hurriedly the American command decided to drop a regiment of paratroops right on to the beachhead to give the Big Red One the support it vitally needed.

The troop carriers from North Africa bearing the 2,000 paratroopers reached the coast of Sicily at the same time that a great V of German bombers, surrounded by a mass of fighters, appeared over Gela to launch the first German air strike against the new beachhead. A tremendous dog-fight commenced as the Allied fighters took up the challenge. Immediately the sky above Gela became a dizzy frightening kaleidoscope of Axis and Allied fighters snarling to and fro in tight, ear-splitting turns, their machine-guns and cannon chattering, streaking the heavens with red, white and green tracer, intermingled with the black puffballs of exploding anti-aircraft shells.

Hurriedly the fleet anchored off the shore put to sea, leaving the beachhead to the trapped infantry watching from their hurriedly dug foxholes the tremendous air battle taking place above their heads.

It was then that the 144 transport planes bearing the paras started to appear above the fleet, heading for their DZs, their recognition lights winking to identify them to the great fleet below, as it rode out the air-raid on the calm blue waters of the Mediterranean.

Then tragedy struck. A lone machine-gun opened up. White tracer started to curve upwards at the DC-47s, gathering speed by the instant, as the transports came ever lower. Immediately the pilots started to flash their recognition signals. Aldis lamps flashed their warnings. To no avail. That lone machine-gun seemed to act as a signal to the rest of the US fleet. Everywhere the ships' anti-aircraft guns erupted into violent action. Heavy cannon boomed. Multiple machine guns chattered frenetically.

The slow majestic transports flying almost at mast-height hadn't a chance. Like a covey of startled quail the squadrons split as the frantic pilots twisted and turned trying to escape that deadly fire. Already some of the pilots had alerted their paras to the extreme danger they were in. Doors were flung open. Tight sticks of paras started to tumble out of the twisting aircraft, falling to certain drowning, weighed down as they were by one hundred pounds of equipment.

A crippled transport came streaming down, trailing bright red fire behind it, both engines shattered. Somehow the pilot, fighting desperately behind his shattered perspex screen, brought her down to crash-land on the sea next to an American destroyer. Immediately the jubilant captain of the American ship ordered his guns into action. As the survivors scrambled on to the waterlogged wing, happy to have been saved after all, they were swept by gunfire from their own ship.

Everywhere it was the same. On the hard-pressed beach, rage, sorrow and hysteria reigned. But there was nothing the infantrymen could do to prevent the slaughter of the airborne reinforcements. Then the slaughter was over. Fifty of the planes had been shot down or badly damaged, over two hundred of the paratroopers had been killed or wounded, and a whole airborne regiment had been strewn over such a large area that the soldiers would be no use to the Big Red One; and as the guns finally fell silent, one by one, realizing their mistake at last, leaving behind them a loud echoing brooding silence, the sea all around was filled with the heavy log-like shapes of what had once been men, nudged gently back and forth by the unheeding waves. This was the situation off Gela as the Commanding General of the Seventh US Army, George S. Patton Junior, prepared to make his ceremonial entry into Sicily.

FIVE

Roaring Red Rory Mulligan sweated as he ran up and down the debris-littered beach, stumbling over the abandoned lifebelts which lay everywhere like fat white slugs. 'Get them kleig lights ready!' he cried. 'You, A-A gunners set them helmets straight! Cameramen – get right down to the water's edge so that the General will look taller when he comes wading ashore. Christ on a crutch, have I to tell you guys everything?' he moaned as the landing craft bearing the General and his staff nosed its way ever closer through the bodies of the dead paras. *'Goddammit, this is fucking history!'*

Above the beach at the entrance to the deep cave in which they had spent that terrible morning, Otto, the Count and the two OSS officers, red-eyed, unshaven and very hungry, watched the preparations taking place below with the stupid uncomprehending looks on their faces of men who are very, very weary and can only take things in slowly. 'It's him,' Friar Tuck concluded finally, rubbing his dirty hand across his scummed cracked parched lips. 'The General, I mean.'

It seemed to take the others a goodly while before they could absorb the information. Below some of Roaring Red Rory's helpers were dragging up two dead Italian soldiers through the scuffed sand and posing them dramatically at the water's edge at the spot where the General would land. 'Put the wop's arms up above his head, willya!' Red Rory's angry shout came wafting up towards them. 'For crying out loud, the guy looks as if he died of old age the way you've got him, not from a slug through the nuts!'

'What do you think, Friar?' the Count asked hesitantly. 'Should we report ourselves to Colonel Mulligan – and the General?'

Friar Tuck looked slightly unhappy. 'I don't think we're gonna be particularly welcome down there at this moment, Count,' he answered after a moment's consideration. 'I mean we made a snafu of our assignment, didn't we?'

'Snafu, Friar?'

'Situation normal – all fucked up!' Friar answered the Count's query a little unhappily.

'Come on, come on, guys,' Red Rory's impassioned cry came floating up from the beach. 'Get the lead outa ya butts! The General's gonna hit the beach in a minute. You, the guy with eye-glasses, on camera one, get ready to dolly around. I wanna a background shot of the whole beach as he comes ashore, and for Chrissake, don't forget that burning Kraut truck over there near the dunes! You on two, let's get the looks of enthusiasm and all that kinda crap on the faces of those A-A[1] boys as they recognize who it is. Three . . .'

'I think the best thing would be,' Friar Tuck broke into the sound of Red Rory's rasping irate voice, 'to let that big Irish Colonel down there get his show on the road and see what kinda look ole Blood an' Guts has got on his face when he steps ashore. If he looks mad, let's wait for him to cool off a bit before we report in—'

'*Roll 'em!*' Red Rory's excited command cut into his words. '*Here he comes!*'

General Patton, still unaware of the dire situation of his Big Red One, had dressed himself fittingly for the great occasion. He was groomed immaculately in his best boots, uniform, his necktie firmly knotted and tucked neatly into his shirt underneath the second button. His pistols rested at his side in open holsters, while a map-case and outsize

[1] anti-aircraft

binoculars dangled from his chest. Beneath the gleaming helmet with its three gold stars, a huge cigar jutted from his thin cruel lips set in his William the Conqueror cum Julius Caesar Crossing the Rubicon Face.

Now he prepared to get over the side of the bobbing craft. To his front a team of MPs, most of them wearing sunglasses, but all bearing tommy guns, dropped into the water and began to wade ashore, gazes flashing from left to right suspiciously. Patton looked at his expensive Hamilton chronometer on his right wrist. 'Zero nine hundred thirty precisely,' he announced to his waiting staff. 'Gentlemen, here we go!' He clambered over the side. Almost as if signalled, artillery from the Hermann Goering positions beyond the hills opened up. The still air was ripped apart like a huge piece of canvas being torn. One . . . two . . . three . . . The massive hundred pound shells from an 88mm cannon came howling down and exploded in great spouts of boiling angry white water some thirty metres away from the General's boat.

Red Rory was beside himself with joy. He danced up and down on the sand in unrestrained pleasure. '*Great . . . great!*' he chortled. '*Oh, brother, get it all . . . the whole works!*'

Squinting majestically Patton walked straight towards the whirring cameras, paused momentarily to survey a couple of wrecked landing craft, turning his face to the right so that the Signals Corps photographers could take his masterly profile, then came out of the water, stamping his feet and grinning mischievously, as if he knew exactly just what a ham he was at such moments.

But his grin was not fated to last for very long.

'How did I do, Red?' he cried above the noise.

Roaring Red Rory touched his hand to his helmet and cried back, 'Swell, General, just swell! A week from now there won't be a movie theatre from east to west coast where they won't be showing you landing here.'

Patton rubbed his jaw reflectively. 'Well, it ain't exactly

a pretty mug, Red, but it's been well lived in,' he began, when abruptly the German 88mm cannon opened up again and to the rear of the beach, sand spurted high into the air, in the same instant that a panic-stricken voice screamed, '*Tanks . . . Kraut tanks heading this way!*'

General Patton forgot Red and his movie crew immediately. He sprang on to the deck of the scout-car which was to take him off the beach to Gela and hurriedly focused his outsize binoculars.

Some eight hundred yards away a half dozen black squat shapes were nosing their way cautiously through the fog of war towards the beach. Behind them, only just glimpsed through the smoke, there were others, many others, all heading with slow mechanical determination for the American beachhead. 'Hot shit,' Patton exclaimed excitedly, in no way afraid at the sight of the enemy so close, 'they really are krauts!' He dropped the glasses to his immaculately uniformed chest. 'You, sailor,' he called to the young ensign with a walkie-talkie who had just appeared. 'Hey, you with the radio!'

The naval officer said smartly, 'Can I help you, sir?'

'You sure as hell can,' Patton snapped, as the first German tanks started to take the dunes now, all seven of them, their guns pointing straight at the petrified engineers and sailors unloading stores from the barges. 'If you can connect with your goddam Navy tell them for God's sake to drop some shell fire on that goddam road.' He pointed at the road along which the first seven tanks were advancing. 'Pronto.'

The ensign's face went white. 'Oh my God!' he blurted out and then hurriedly he fumbled with his instrument, while Patton tapped his fingers nervously against his binoculars and behind him the cameramen started to dig a hiding place with unprecedented speed for such 'artists'.

'I've got the *Boise*, sir,'[1] the ensign exclaimed suddenly.

[1] A US cruiser

'She's going to let them have a salvo from her six-inch guns in—'

The rest of his words were drowned by the tremendous roar of ship's artillery. On the horizon, sudden pink flashes stabbed the fog and smoke. '*Incoming mail!*' someone roared as the six-inch gun shells ripped flatly through the sullen sky, howled over the heads of the gaping Americans, and smashed down with an earth-shaking detonation right on the tanks, throwing them into the air like toys.

'*Hot shit!*' Patton cried and danced up and down on the deck of the scout car with joy. 'Now we've really got them by the nose and a boot up the ass!'

It was thus while General Patton personally directed the defence of the beach that a lone jeep came racing across the dunes, zig-zagging wildly in great flurries of sand between shell-bursts, narrowly missing four lone civilians wearily plodding towards Patton, heads bent as if they were advancing against a fierce wind. It braked in a wake of sand. General Allen, commander of the Big Red One, and his Corps Commander General Omar Bradley, a tall bespectacled, heavy-jawed officer, clambered out hurriedly and saluted a happy Patton, who stood directing the counter-fire, obviously enjoying every moment of it, in spite of the danger.

After a few minutes, with the surviving German tanks scuttling back the way they had come, leaving behind their wrecked, fiercely burning comrades, Patton deigned to notice the two Generals standing below him. 'All right, Terry and you Brad,' he yelled above the howl of the shells, 'at ease.' He grinned down at their weary, serious faces. 'What's matter with you guys? You both look as if you just got your dongs caught in the wringer!'

But this day even Patton's coarse humour could not raise a smile from his two subordinates; the situation was too serious.

'Okay, feed it to me, Brad,' Patton's smile vanished. 'Where's the goddam fire?'

'Everywhere, George,' Bradley said in his plaintive Missouri accent.

'What the goddam hell do ya mean?'

'Terry's First here is taking a bad beating from the other feller, George.'

Allen nodded his agreement and sighed wearily. 'The Hermann Goering has gotten right into my positions. The positions of my 18th Regiment have been infiltrated in strength. My 16th Regiment seems to be disintegrating on the Niscemi road, and the situation of the rest of my Division doesn't look exactly rosy, George.'

Patton absorbed the information for a moment and then snorted angrily, 'Gentlemen, there are gonna be no gloomy faces in this Army. Okay, my little plan to have the Hermann Goering sicced on to Monty didn't work. Right, then regard it as an honour, Terry, to be tackling the finest outfit the Krauts have on Sicily.' He held up his hands, as if he were forming a pot in mid-air. 'Look at it like this. So now they're right into your positions, Allen. Excellent, the Krauts have stuck their heads right into the meat-grinder. It's up to us to turn the handle and turn 'em into grade A hamburger meat.' His voice rose, as if he were addressing a public meeting and he put on his Abe Lincoln Giving the Gettysburg Address in 1863 Face. 'Everyone in this Army must understand that we are not fighting this battle in any half-cocked way. It's either roothog or die. If those sons of bitches want war in the raw, then that's the way we'll give it to them!' He dropped his pose and started to rap out a series of orders to a suddenly renewed General Allen, ending with, 'Everyone stays just where he is! Under no circumstances will anyone be pulled back!'

Allen beamed up at him. 'You can rely on the Big Red One, sir,' he exclaimed.

Patton grinned at him with his dingy, worn-down teeth. 'You betcha, I can, Terry,' he barked, 'or else I'm gonna bust your arse down to buck private and you'll be on the shit-shovelling detail for the next twenty years!'

'Now it was General Allen's turn to grin.

'Okay, on your way, Terry, and get those heroes of yours back on the stick.'

Patton waited till General Allen had sprinted back to his jeep, where the driver anxious to get away was already gunning his engine, before turning to Bradley. 'Okay, Brad, first give me the bad news. That little fart Montgomery landed without opposition didn't he?'

Bradley nodded gloomily. Behind them the firing had died away altogether and the supply boats were busily dumping their stores once more. Someone was saying miserably, 'But this is already the fourth wave and those goddam rubbers of mine haven't been landed yet!' 'There were a few Eyeties there to meet him, Georgie, but all they did was to fire a salute of honour and then surrender. It was a walk-over for the Eighth Army.'

'Go on, Brad,' Patton said, 'don't spare me. Give me the whole miserable details.'

'According to our Intelligence, he occupied Syracuse at zero nine hundred hours this morning, and the Eyeties have abandoned it without any attempt to wreck the harbour installations. Not only that, this midday the Royal Navy sailed into the harbour at Augusta even before British troops had arrived in the town. That means—'

'That means Monty, the little squirt, has got two major ports to supply him and I'm still stuck on my arse on this open beach, pinned down by the Krauts with not a harbour or port facility within grabbing distance.'

Bradley nodded gloomily, 'That's about it, George.'

Patton absorbed the information for a few moments, then said, 'Brad, gimme your map.'

Dutifully Bradley handed his superior the map of Sicily and Patton spread it on the deck of the scout car. For a few moments he stared hard at it before saying, 'My educated guess, Brad, is that this is what's gonna happen in the next few days. Montgomery, now he's got the ports and can build up his supplies and troops rapidly, will start pushing towards Messina by two diverging paths. The first'll follow the rim of the island – here – up the eastern coast road, across the marshes, through Catania and beyond it along the narrow shelf of land – here – between Mount Etna and the sea. The second'll run through the hub – here – north of Mount Etna towards Messina.'

Bradley nodded his agreement.

'For our part, Brad, we will be confined to the western part of the island until we reach the coast, where more than likely we will be told to halt.'

Bradley tugged at the end of his long nose gloomily. 'Yeah, George, once we've cleared this mess up here on the beachhead, I guess that will be our lot and I don't think there is much glory gonna be gained capturing a lot of useless scenery, dumb peasants and docile soldiers so that we can sit comfortably on our prats on the coast while Monty gets Messina and finishes the goddam war.'

'Exactly,' Patton agreed, but there was no dismay on his face. Bradley noted the cunning gleam in his superior's eyes and said, 'You've gotten something up your sleeve, George, haven't you?'

Patton took his time replying. 'Not exactly, Brad. But as Monty has had an easy landing, has gotten those two ports and it is already clear to the Krauts what his final objective is, what do you think the – other fellow, as you always call the Krauts – will do?'

Now it was Bradley's turn to take his time. 'Why, George, I guess,' he said finally, 'he'll put as much strength as he can find into stopping Monty.'

'Exactly – and where is he going to find that strength? I'll tell you, Brad.' Patton answered his own question, pointing to the horizon, its smoke-covered outlines split repeatedly by the scarlet flashes and stabs of cannonfire. 'There. As far as the Krauts are concerned we are not the main threat, simply an amusing side-show, nothing to be taken seriously. They've already given us a bloody nose on the beaches. Okay,' he shrugged easily, 'they reason that

THE RACE FOR MESSINA, JULY 1943

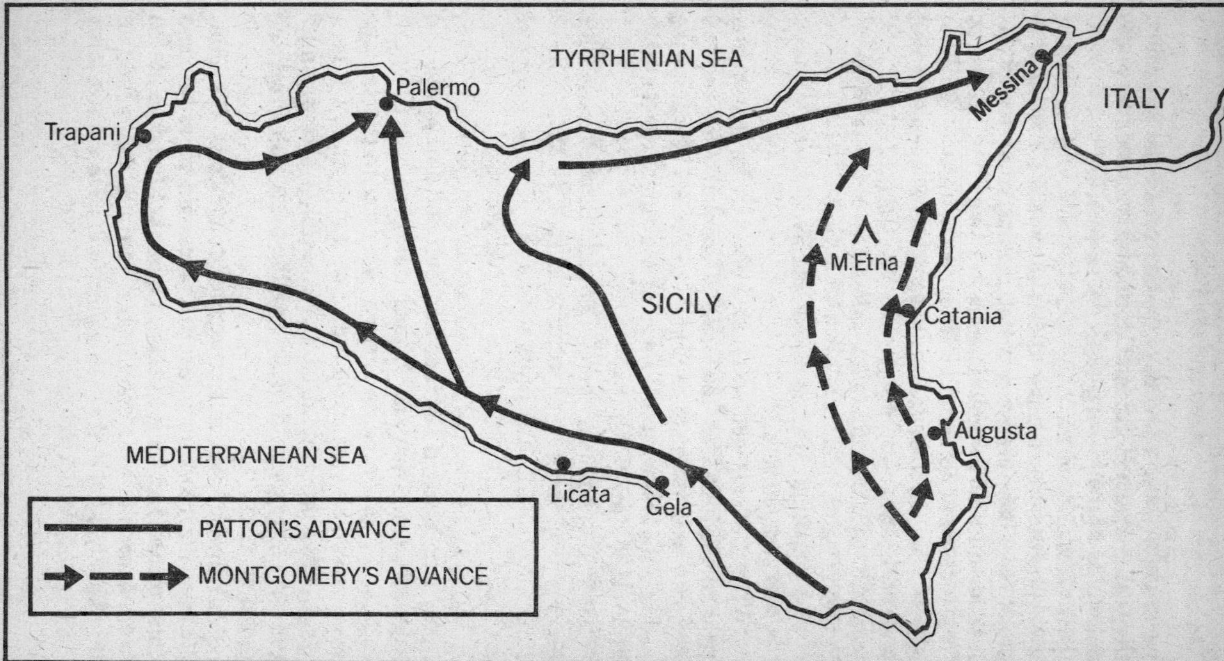

we're gonna take a few days to recover. In the meantime they can ease the Hermann Goering boys out and leave the defending of the hinterland to the wops.'

Bradley nodded his agreement eagerly. 'Of course, it would be the logical thing to do and typical for them. The other feller was always great at making most use of his interior lines of communication and switching his troops from one front to another. They learnt that in the First World War.' His sudden smile vanished as soon as it had appeared. 'But that don't help us, George. We're still confined to this miserable side-show here in Western Sicily.'

'Are we, Brad?' Patton asked blandly.

'What do you mean?'

'What if Monty gets so bogged down along that coastal road to Messina that the brass – Ike and Alex back in Algiers – start to squawk? What if somebody else grabs the ball and makes the touch down at Messina instead of that little limey shit? What if—'

'Hold on, hold on there, George!' Bradley raised his hand to stop the flow of words. 'As soon as Montgomery runs into trouble, the brass will order us to step up our activities to take the pressure off Montgomery.'

Patton smiled cunningly. 'Once we're in the field, Brad, there'll be many a slip between cup and lip, as the old saying has it. Okay, so Algiers starts sending us coded orders. We get decoding delayed. We pretend the message was garbled and ask for a repeat of the original. Oh hell, Brad, there are a hundred and one things a commander can do, once he's in the field and the brass isn't breathing down his neck.'

Still Bradley was not altogether convinced. 'All right, George, I agree with you up to a certain point. A field commander does have a certain amount of freedom of that kind if he plays his cards right, but still the weight of numbers will tell in the end. Monty will have a whole army ashore by the end of this week to fight against two or three German divisions. He'll do it in the end.'

'Sure, but while he's slogging it out with the Krauts we'll be barrelling through the wops like a dose of salts through a Mexican's greasy guts ready to move on Messina at a moment's notice.'

'But—'

'No buts, Brad. I'm gonna pull out all the stops to ensure that Monty does not make Messina before my Seventh. The prestige of the United States Army is at stake. We're gonna get there first by hell or highwater!'

'But how, George?' Bradley cried in exasperation. 'For Chrissake, tell me *how*?'

By way of answer, Patton pointed at the four sorry-looking civilians, one of whom appeared to be a monk or friar or something of that sort, grouped miserably near Colonel Mulligan, who for some reason known only to himself was looking very grim. 'See those jerks,' he cried harshly. 'They're the ones who are gonna stop the limeys or by God I swear I'll put the lot of them in Leavenworth for the rest of their born days![1] *Dismiss . . .*'

[1] Fort Leavenworth, military prison reserved for serious military criminals

SIX

In that third week of July 1943, strange things happened along the eastern coast of Sicily as Montgomery's vaunted 'desert rats' slowly but surely started to push the Germans back towards Messina.

An armoured column, for example, would find in front of its lead tank what appeared to be a straight run, the blue and white signpost at the road side clearly indicating the way ahead; but after an hour or so the straight white road, built in the twenties by the Fascists, would end up in a rocky gorge without any exit. More and more vehicles would pile up after it creating a monumental traffic jam that took hours to unscramble.

More than once a POL dump[1] which provided the life-blood of an armoured drive would be inexplicably hit by mortar fire out of the surrounding hills, although later red-faced Intelligence officers swore that the Germans had long vanished from their positions up there; or there would be a mysterious flash-fire at night, usually blamed in the end, after fruitless inquiries, on some careless RASC sentry, tossing away his cigarette end while on sentry go.

There was, too, the notorious case of a whole convoy of three-ton trucks, rushing up to the hard-pressed front with a supply of 25 pounder ammunition, vitally needed if the artillery were to winkle out some grenadiers of the Hermann Goering from a hill position. Suddenly, one after another came to a miserable halt, steam jetting from their radiators, their pistons, as the irate drivers soon discovered, completely seized up. It was only after careful examination

[1] Petrol and oil storage points

by the specialists of the REME, who in full view of the German riflemen and beneath the blazing Sicilian sun stripped more than ten big engines to discover that someone had poured sugar into them.

For twenty-four hours the whole army, some 100,000 men strong, was held by a suspected minefield laid between two dominating hill features to both right and left of the single coastal road until finally a company of Royal Engineers volunteered to take up the minefield. 'It's twenty-eight days in the glass-house if you *don't* volunteer,' their company commander had appealed earlier that day to their patriotic sentiments – 'and three bottles of any Eyetie brew you fancy, if you *do*.' Red-eyed, angry and bewildered they had reported back to the lines of the tense, anxiously waiting infantry the following dawn, bearing with them dinner plates. 'Buckets of blood,' the infantry commander had cursed, scarlet with anger, dashing the plate, a rather attractive native design at that, to the stony ground, 'it's more than a chap can bear! What cunning swine these Huns are, making a pseudo-minefield out of a wog's tea set!'

The very next day the whole army ground to a miserable halt yet once again when the lead battalion abruptly went sick with a violent case of 'gippo tummy', moaning and groaning, rolling around in the dust and rocks in their agony, littering a two square miles area with the products of their inflamed bowels. Indeed that particular day, while a fresh infantry battalion edged its way through the massive pile-up of honking, hooting vehicles to take over the point, a special plane was flown in from Augusta bearing nothing but Army Form Bumpf. The stricken battalion had run out of the coarse brown army lavatory paper and their CO had moaned over the radio, his message obviously understood by the waiting Germans dug in in the hills ahead, 'Battalion run out of grass sods for cleansing . . . Send bumpf at once . . . or it's the end!'

Some time later back at Syracuse the scientists of the Royal Army Medical Corps discovered during their clinical tests that the day's tea ration of the battalion had been treated by a powerful laxative, normally used in Sicily to relieve acute constipation in mules. The finding had resulted in consternation throughout that veteran army. Shocked desert rats, who had fought back and forth across the Western Desert since 1940 and had gone through hell, whispered the news to each other that night in hushed tones usually reserved for the football results, '*Someone's poisoned the char! Christ, how low can the Jerries sink!*'

Worse was still to come when one of the mobile propaganda armoured cars interrupted its metallic broadcast to the entrenched Germans somewhere up front, cutting into a rendition of Vera Lynn singing about her celebrated 'Nightingale in Berkeley Square' to announce in English, 'It's all over, boys! The Jerries have surrendered! Everyone is to hold in place. The Jerries have surrendered. Official . . . *Surrendered!*' The excited voice died away to be replaced by a spirited recording of Billy Cotton's band playing the '*Hokey-Cokey*'.

To the strains of '*yer put yer left foot in, yer put yer left foot out, yer shake it all around,*' the lead battalion broke out the rum ration for the day, the fat quartermaster personally serving it to the happy relaxed companies. By midday Monday's ration had vanished. Tuesday's and Wednesday's followed soon. By the time an irate infantry brigadier reached the front in his jeep to discover why his lead battalion was making no progress, with Montgomery screaming over the phone for action, he found three-quarters of the battalion stretched out blind drunk in the white-hot Sicilian afternoon sunshine and the CO and the Quartermaster (wearing his favourite drag costume normally reserved for Saturday evenings when the battalion was not in action) doing a dreamy cheek-to-cheek slow foxtrot together in the shade afforded by some olive trees . . .

*

'It's weally not quite on, Blackie,' Montgomery said severely, touching the pile of reports on the desk in front of him in the hot caravan, which he had looted from an Italian general in the desert the previous year, 'doctored engines, poisoned tea and now this beastly business with the rum. I mean I am the last person, as you know, to start belly-aching. But I think this really is the limit.'

Ever since Otto had knocked out his teeth, and not having yet found replacements in Sicily, Colonel Blackie Burrows tended to say very little, and when he did speak, he scarcely opened his mouth, making him look grim-faced and anxious and hardly audible.

Blackie nodded. 'I've seen it all before, sir,' he mumbled.

Montgomery looked at him in surprise. 'All before?'

'Yessir. On the North West Frontier.'

'You mean the wily Pathan?' Montgomery asked, his eyes narrowing thoughtfully.

'Exactly, sir.'

'But there aren't any Pathans around here,' Montgomery objected after a moment. 'Or at least, I don't think there are.'

'I shouldn't imagine so, sir,' Blackie agreed. 'No, the swine who carried out these dastardly attacks are white men. By colour, I mean, sir,' Blackie added hastily, 'not by nature.'

'You mean you know who did this?'

'I have my suspicions, sir,' a tight-lipped Blackie replied. 'I think all these things were done to slow down your drive to Messina.'

Montgomery looked up at the Colonel aghast. 'I say, Blackie, you don't think . . .' he stuttered.

'Let us say, sir,' Blackie said, 'that I am making an educated guess about who's behind this nasty business. That's why I asked to see you, sir, in order to request permission to do something about it.'

Montgomery squinted up at the Colonel in the oblique rays of the afternoon sun, feeling its heat penetrate his thin khaki shirt. 'You've got it, Blackie,' he said, telling himself it was not wise to pursue the matter any further with the Colonel. He trusted the small staff of his little tactical HQ, but gossip travelled fast and it wouldn't do at all, if it came out that he suspected Patton of attempting to throw a spanner in the works. 'Bowl them out leg-before-wicket, if you follow me.'

'I do, sir,' Blackie said with tight-lipped grimness. 'I do indeed. I'll make the swine pay, after all I've got an old score to pay back.'

'Good then, off you go and knock 'em for six, Blackie.' Montgomery waved a skinny hand with feigned cheefulness at his subordinate and stepped back into the Italian general's caravan.

It was cooler inside and he poured himself a glass of lukewarm water before he sat down on the bunk to stare at the large framed photographs of his erstwhile enemies, which he kept on the walls of his caravan to remind him that he was facing real men not just abstract creatures labelled the 'enemy'. At least that is what he told the usual admiring press correspondents whenever he gave a conference, which was often. It was a good publicity stunt, and it seemed to cheer them up; it was a bit of copy at all events.

He sipped the water, as if it were rare vintage wine and sank into a lazy mid-afternoon reverie, oblivious to the rattle of typewriters outside and the ring of telephones. Once he winked at Rommel's stern Swabian face. Next to him the photograph of Field-Marshal Albert Kesselring, known by his troops as 'Smiling Albert', seemed to wink back, a happy look on his beefy red face. The impression pleased Montgomery. He sat back more comfortably on the narrow bunk.

So Patton was behind the events of the last few days, eh, he mused to himself, recalling the cunning look he had spotted on his rival's face back in that African bog, the month before. He wouldn't put it past him. It was a typical

Yank trick. They'd do anything for headlines. Sometimes he thought that all their senior generals were only in the war to obtain enough publicity so that they could run for president in civvie street. Ike was always wanting to be photographed kissing babies and slapping private soldiers on the shoulder heartily, his face split from ear to ear in a smile. For a moment Montgomery, dreaming there in the hot caravan, wished that they had a president back in the UK so that he could run for the office himself; he'd probably make a jolly good one, he told himself.

Again he concentrated on Patton, visualizing his lean poseur's face. Suddenly, in his mind's eye, it was transformed into a poached egg. The sight pleased him immensely, although he felt a little sorry for the Yank. But it served him right, he told himself. Indeed it was shamefully agreeable that Patton might believe too one day that he was a poached egg.

For a while he indulged his fantasy with a mental vision of a harassed Patton working his way down a line of high-ranking Allied generals telling each of them that he was a poached egg and asking them humbly if they hadn't a piece of toast about their persons upon which he might rest his delicate white and yellow substance.

Montgomery shook his head and pulling out his khaki-coloured handkerchief dabbed his dripping brow, the Sicilian sunshine was hotter than he thought, perhaps there was something to be said for the old pre-war solar topee. Patton as a poached egg vanished swiftly to be replaced by Rommel and 'Smiling Albert'.

It was just then that he became aware of the sudden commotion outside and the sound of heavy army boots running across the hard-baked earth to his caravan. Someone gave a thunderous knock on his door.

'Come!' he called.

It was young Freddie Carruthers of the 'Cherrypickers', who worked with old Blackie, his face flushed crimson, sweat gleaming in the sweep of his big black cavalry moustache. 'Sir . . . sir,' he gasped, too excited or shocked even to salute. 'Something terrible has happened.'

'Well, out with it, boy! What?'

'Sir, sir,' Carruthers stuttered. 'Whoever's attempting to sabotage our drive north has just blown up two NAAFI vans on the pass road near Etna. No one's hurt fortunately, but the whole road is blocked with spam wads and rock buns . . . baked beans and the like. Of course the infantry have downed tools and are tucking in for all they're worth while the sappers get the road cleared. They say it'll take twelve hours before they finish it and Brigadier Currie who's up there with the infantry reports he'll have a devil of a job prying them loose from the rock buns . . .' Carruthers' voice trailed away to nothing, as he watched the 'Master's' (for that was what he was called by his admiring young officers) face flush purple with suppressed rage.

Finally Montgomery spoke, obviously controlling himself with the greatest of difficulty. 'By God, Freddie,' he said in a shaky voice, 'I wish he would turn into a poached egg after this dastardly outrage!'

'Yessir,' Carruthers replied dutifully, wondering who 'he' was and why and how he should turn into a 'poached egg' of all things, telling himself that the shock must have been too much for the 'Master'; he'd gone a little doolally. He backed out without another word, leaving Montgomery sunk deep in thought, little realizing that the unknown 'he' would soon get himself into a situation where he would dearly love to be a poached egg or even a scrambled one for that matter – anything indeed but Lt General George S. Patton, Junior . . .

SEVEN

The downfall of General George S. Patton started the very same day that a weary sunburnt Otto, the Count and the two American OSS men came to report to him the success of their latest attempt to sabotage the British drive to the north. As usual the General was out visiting his troops and they caught up with him as he was visiting the wounded at 9th General Hospital, a frontline tented evacuation hospital located in a valley near the Sicilian village of Sant' Agata di Militello.

While Lt Al Cheetham, who was fond of his food, chewed stolidly on one of the ironhard rock buns which they had picked up at the spot where they had mined the two NAAFI vans, much to the surprise of the two middle-aged English lesbians who drove them and had gone off to relieve themselves in the cover of the rocks near the coastal road, Patton followed by his entourage walked from litter to litter, handing out Purple Hearts to the wounded GIs. Otto followed his progress with interest, admiring the trouble the tall skinny American General took with the half-naked men squinting up at him in the sun, asking the same old question, but with a new intonation of stress for each one of them; it was a performance in itself.

'Where did you get it boy?' he would ask softly.

'In the chest', or 'in the head, sir', they would reply, and immediately Patton's voice would rise, become bellicose and he would snort, 'Well, son, it might interest you to know that the last Kraut sonavabitch I saw had no head nor chest, too, for that matter. Get well quick, son – I want you to be in at the kill in Messina.'

Once he even got a laugh when he asked a coal-black Negro the same old question, 'Where did you get it, boy?' 'In de bivouac area, sah,' the coloured man replied in all seriousness.

The last wounded GI was unconscious again, someone of the hospital staff had obviously slipped up – the General only wanted to see wounded who could respond. But General Patton did not bat an eyelid. He did a quick switch. Taking off his helmet he went down on one knee to pin the medal on the soldier's blood-stained shirt; then he whispered a few words into his ear. When he rose half the hard-boiled female nurses were sobbing gently and even the chief-surgeon was blowing his nose with unaccustomed force.

Otto shook his head in mock admiration. General Patton, ham as he was, certainly knew how to entertain his military audiences. But then the situation changed dramatically. Suddenly Patton noticed a helmetless soldier squatting next to the entrance of the nearest big hospital tent, nervously puffing at a *Camel* held in a hand which trembled violently. The young GI wore no bloodstained bandage like the rest, nor did he have the usual wound-tag attached to his olive-drab shirt. Patton frowned and stepped to him. 'What brought you here, boy?' he snapped.

'I'm running a temperature, sir,' the nervous ashen-faced GI replied.

'Yessir,' a nearby doctor in a blood-stained white overall chimed in swiftly, as if to protect the GI, 'it's a little over 102 degrees, sir.'

Patton raised his eyebrows obviously not convinced that a soldier running a temperature should be taking up a valuable space in an evacuation hospital. But he said nothing more, for his eyes had fallen on another soldier, trembling even more violently than the one with the cigarette, 'What's your trouble?' he snapped, staring down in distaste at the man sitting there, arms huddled around his skinny body. 'Well?'

The soldier flashed him a look. 'It's my nerves, General!' he replied and then lowering his head he began to sob, his thin shoulders heaving like a broken-hearted child.

'What the Sam Hill did you say?' Patton shrieked, his thin face suddenly flushing a hectic red.

Lt Cheetham dropped his rock bun hurriedly, alarmed by the look on Patton's face. 'Christ,' he whispered to Otto, 'now the shit is really gonna hit the fan!'

'It's my nerves, General,' the boy sobbed, the tears running down his skinny yellow face without restraint. 'I can't stand the shelling. I just can't!' He dropped his head once more, his sobs growing in intensity.

Otto swallowed hard. Patton's rage was impressive to see, for he had drawn himself up to his full height, his lean body rigid, gloved hands clenched in tight fists, held stiffly at his side. 'Your nerves!' he exploded, head twisted to one side, voice strangled, face a fiery red. 'Hell, you're just a . . . a goddamn coward! You . . . you yellow son-of-a-bitch!' Suddenly his right hand flew out, and caught the sobbing boy a stinging blow across the cheek so that his head swung to one side.

There was a shocked intake of breath from the spectators. Patton did not seem to hear it. 'Shut up that goddamned crying!' he shrieked in his high-pitched voice, furious and trembling now with rage. 'I won't have these brave men here who have been shot seeing a yellow bastard sitting here crying!'

'General!' one of the white-coated doctors called warningly, '*please!*'

But Patton was beyond paying heed to warnings. His hand lashed out again. The sobbing man's helmet liner flew off and rolled to a stop in front of the next tent. Patton swung round to the Receiving Officer, the doctor who allotted wounded and sick men to the hospital. 'You,' he cried, 'don't you admit this yellow bastard!'

'But General—' the doctor began nervously.

Patton cut his protest short. 'There's nothing the matter

with him. I won't have the hospitals cluttered up with these sons of bitches who haven't got the guts to fight.' Patton swung round on the soldier he had struck once more. 'You,' he snarled, 'you're going back to the front lines and you may get shot and killed, but you're gonna *fight*! If you don't, I'll stand you against a wall and have a firing squad shoot you. In fact,' Patton lowered his voice menacingly, dropping his hand to his ivory-handled pistol, 'I ought to shoot you myself, you goddamned whimpering coward!'

Next to Otto, Al Cheetham caught his breath and Otto, who couldn't take his gaze off the drama being enacted before his eyes heard him gasp, 'Oh, no, for Chrissake, *not that!*'

On all sides the doctors tensed, as if they were preparing to spring in between the crimson-faced General and the sobbing ashen-faced boy kneeling on the ground, hands clasped together above his cropped head in the classic pose of supplication.

Somehow or other, Patton caught himself just in time. He breathed out hard and while the onlookers stared at his right hand with hypnotic fascination, he slowly withdrew it from the fancy pistol. He strode back towards his waiting scout car, striding past Otto, the Count and the two OSS men without a glance in their direction, followed by a grim-faced hospital director Colonel Currier. Just before he clambered up into the gleaming turret of the vehicle, he turned round on the doctor and rasped, 'Colonel, I meant what I said about getting that coward out there. I won't have those cowardly bastards hanging around our hospitals. We'll probably have to shoot them sometime anyway, or we'll raise a breed of morons!' He touched his hand to his helmet as if in salute, though the shocked Colonel had not offered him that form of military respect. Easily he swung himself into the turret. The driver started the motor immediately as if glad to escape from the tent hospital. With the sirens going full blast, as was Patton's custom, the little column swept away down the valley road, Patton standing grim and erect in the turret, eyes fixed on some distant horizon known only to himself.

The doctors, the nurses relaxed, all save the hospital director Colonel Currier. 'Get that man out of the ambulance and re-admit him,' he snapped to the two nurses who had hurriedly hidden the boy Patton had slapped in the back of a bullet-pocked ambulance, as if they had feared that the General might well return and carry out his threat to shoot him. He strode over to the desk of the Receiving Officer standing out in the open in the bright Sicilian sunshine. Angrily, beside himself with rage as well now, he whirled the handle of the field telephone and waited impatiently until he could talk. 'Hello,' he snapped, 'this Currier of the 94th Evac . . . Second Corps HQ? . . . Yes . . . Hello, there, sir . . . There has been a serious incident here . . . No, sir, I don't want to talk about it over the phone . . . I suggest, sir, that you'd better come over here as fast as you can make it, sir. Thank you, sir.' He slammed down the phone and glared at the silent expectant medical staff. 'So what are you standing about for?' he cried. 'You've got casualties to treat, haven't you? Get on with the job now. The fun and games are over – for the time being . . .'

Captain Wipem spat contemptuously into the parched grass. 'So what's *his* beef?' he asked with a sneer, indicating the angry Colonel stalking off to his own duties. 'The General was right. That yellow-livered bastard deserved all he got – and then some! A little corporal punishment never hurt anybody.'

Lt Al Cheetham shook his head sadly. 'There you're wrong, Wipem,' he said slowly and reflectively, 'that punishment is really gonna hurt this time – and for good.'

The Captain looked at Cheetham's plump good-natured, features. 'Piss or get off the pot, Cheetham, what are you talking about, eh?'

Cheetham took his time. Another column of dusty,

bullet-chipped boxlike ambulances were working their way down the road towards the hospital, in each driver's window a little sign reading, *Priority. Carrying Casualties*, while nurses and corpsmen ran out with litters to meet them. More wounded from the front outside Messina. Otto licked his parched lips a little nervously. He did not like the sight of broken young bodies; after four years of war he had still not grown accustomed to the sight of bold young men turned into whimpering crushed babies by their wounds.

'He's had it, the General, I mean,' Cheetham answered softly, as the medics opened the rear of the first ambulance and the blood, a bright scarlet in the sunshine, started to drip from its floor to the dusty ground. 'He'll capture Messina all right now. But it'll be a hollow victory, believe you me. Ike'll fire him this time . . . Come on, fellers, let's get on with the job.' Miserably the four men started to trail back to their jeep.

EIGHT

Baron von Borkenheim peered out across the narrow strip of water that separated Messina from mainland Italy. Down below on the wrecked dock jetty, littered with the shattered cranes that his engineers had blown up earlier that morning, the rearguard waited impatiently. Beyond in the heights above the city the American cannon had already begun to rumble once more, as the enemy gunners started to range in. It was rumoured too that the Tommies were going to attempt a landing up the coast before nightfall in order to cut off their retreat to the safety of the mainland. They wanted to be off before it was too late. Baron von Borkenheim was motivated, however, by no such fears. He had fought his Hermann Goering division well. The Führer had sent a telegram of congratulations from far away Russia and the fat Luftwaffe Chief after whom the Division was named, *Reichsmarshall* Hermann Goering, had telephoned and told him confidently that there was going to be a piece of 'tin' in this operation after all, although it was officially a defeat.[1]

For a moment standing there on the quay with the American guns rumbling and mumbling in the distance and here and there spurts of flame erupting from the city behind him, the Baron visualized the headlines back in the Reich on the morrow. '*Hero of Sicily is last to leave . . . The Hermann Goering executes brilliant fighting withdrawal . . . Under the command of Gen. v. Borkenheim, the much decorated veteran, the HG fights off all attacks . . .*' He smiled and told himself that the gift-dwarf, Minister of Propa-

[1] A decoration

ganda Goebbels would have a field-day; he would do the Division and himself proud, he was sure of that. The only fly in the ointment was that he had not collected a wound in this campaign. A picture of himself wounded and suffering, heroically bearing his pain as he was supported to the last ferry boat by his adoring soldiers, would have gone down very well indeed, he knew. It could well have meant a corps command for him. After all he was no chicken. If he didn't get his corps soon, before the war ended, that would be that. He would be retired on half-pay as a divisional general. He stamped his good foot down hard on the quay at the thought.

Just off the harbour, another Italian ferry was beginning to sink, sending its panic-stricken military passengers diving into the sea. It was the fourth that afternoon. As always the frightened spaghetti-eaters overloaded their boats in their haste to escape from the approaching Allies.

Baron von Borkenheim dismissed the Italians and the thought of the glamorous wound which would get him his corps. 'Kuno,' he snapped to the infantry captain who was in charge of the rearguard, 'it's about time we were off now.'

'Sir!' the Captain barked and started barking out orders to the waiting infantry, protecting the engineers putting the final touches to the explosive charges which would demolish the rest of the harbour installations within thirty minutes of the last ferry leaving the harbour.

Von Borkenheim nodded his head in approval. 'Orderly,' he said to his last remaining servant – the rest had been killed in the month-long retreat across the island, 'my stomach's acting up again . . . Just going over there to the little house with the heart in the door.' He indicated the Italian WC, which had once been used by the local dockers. 'Keep an eye on the place will you.'

'Of course, sir,' the young blond orderly answered, unslinging his machine-pistol. He stamped his feet apart, a look of grim determination on his young face. Baron von

Borkenheim smiled. The young chap would defend his thunderbox to the last bullet; he was sure of that. Slowly, as if unaware that all around him a world was coming to an end, his cap set at a rakish angle on his shaven skull, Baron von Borkenheim strolled to the latrine.

It was while thus occupied that a lone half-track, dust-covered and heavy with camouflage nets, began to crawl slowly through the mean peeling tenements that bordered the harbour, the man standing behind the heavy machine-gun in the cab swinging it back and forth suspiciously as he eyed the shuttered upper windows, as if he expected fire to erupt from them at any moment.

But it was not rifle-fire which suddenly broke the heavy brooding silence of those baking hot streets. It was the single cry of delight, '*Americanos!*' flung out from an upstairs window, as the shutters were swept open and a fat sweating man in a dirty undershirt recognized the uniform of the four men crouched in the open half-track below.

'*Americanos! . . . the liberators are here! Evviva Patton!*'

Suddenly, running, cheering, men, women and children poured from doors and hallways on all sides. Lt Al Cheetham braked hard, as the frantic Italian civilians swamped the vehicle, flinging themselves at the running-board, grabbing the surprised comrades, ruffling their hair, trying to snatch kisses, feeling their uniforms, as if they needed to assure themselves that these really were the liberators they had waited for so long. Otto let go of the machine-gun, caught completely by surprise as a plump young signora thrust her stomach tightly against his and before she was wrenched away by others attempting to do the same, planted a huge wet kiss on his lips. He hadn't even time or the presence of mind to run his hand up inside the skirt of her short floral dress. Next to him, the Count staggered back, his face suddenly purple and dripping as it was struck by a bunch of carelessly flung muscatel grapes. 'Oh, I say this is going a bit too far!'

Captain I. Wipem, beside himself with rage, raised his

pistol in the air threateningly. 'For God's sake, get out of the way, you damn crazy wops!' he cried. 'We're on a goddam mission, for crying out loud!'

But the enthusiastic joyous Sicilians were not listening to Captain Wipem, nor did they care that the four comrades had the urgent task of reporting to a waiting and very impatient General Patton. Or that the information they were relaying would enable Patton to make his triumphant entry ahead of the British who were also on their way after their secret landing further up the coast.

Otto pulled the trigger of his pistol. Three quick shots cut the air. But the Sicilians obviously thinking the shots indicated the *Americanos* were as overjoyed as they were, threw themselves even more fervently at the scout car.

At the controls Lt Cheetham tried to brush away a middle-aged plump lady in black, who seemingly was trying to open his flies with excited trembling fingers, while to his left an old toothless crone, whose breath smelled like death, was thrusting a bottle of brandy at his open gasping mouth like a fond mother offering a nipple to a greedy infant.

Now from the jetty below, the Germans worked frantically at fixing their demolition charges, while the infantry took cover behind abandoned packing cases and shattered girders and began snapping off bullets at the cheering, crying civilians, who were too swept away by this Latin torrent of emotional relief and wild exuberance to notice.

Cheetham thrust home first gear, choking on the fierce brandy which the old crone was pouring down his throat, making pleased crooning noises all the time. The middle-aged plump lady, hanging over the windscreen tumbled backwards as the vehicle jerked forward. For one long moment his vision was blocked by the sight of a massive rump clad in tight black silk knickers and the half-track careened off a wall, scattering wildly cheering Sicilians everywhere.

Tracer zipped through the air frighteningly, still the old

crone held on to the front of the cab. Angrily Wipem pushed aside the yelling Sicilian next to him and grabbed the machine-gun from Otto's startled hands. '*Sonuva-bitches!*' he hissed at no one in particular and sent a stream of slugs hissing along the jetty and into the water. An engineer screamed. His arms flailing the air wildly, he staggered backwards into the harbour. Another followed the next instant, his chest ripped open bloodily, looking as if someone had just stitched a line of red button-holes along it.

It was too much for the engineers. They started to fling down their pliers and cutters and pelt for the waiting ferry. The infantry captain fired an angry burst as the half-track rattled ever closer. Otto ducked as the slugs howled off the armoured radiator and shattered the bottle in the crone's claw, leaving her still clinging on somehow or other and staring down at the glass in complete bewilderment. Then the German blew a shrill blast on his whistle. His men needed no urging. Hurriedly they broke from their cover and started to back off towards the waiting ferry, firing from the hip as they did so.

Wipem laughed triumphantly. As Otto pushed aside the heavy-bosomed signora who had been sticking her tongue so deep into one ear, he felt she might penetrate the other ear, was now screaming hysterically. Otto whipped the heavy machine-gun around. A blond indecisive-looking boy, standing outside what looked like a latrine to Otto, raised his weapon. Too late. Wipem pressed his trigger first. The machine-gun chattered violently. Tracer stitched the air. Otto could see it clearly, as it struck up little blue sparks the length of the concrete, hurrying death towards the waiting boy. Suddenly he screamed and sank to his knees, his legs a mess of scarlet blood and shattered brilliant white bone. Next instant he flopped down flat on his face with an audible thwack. Otto turned his head away suddenly sickened, while Wipem cried in sadistic exuberance. 'And another pesky redskin bites the dust!'

'Aw knock it off!' Cheetham snarled, desperately trying to avoid running over the dying boy. But that wasn't to be. A stick grenade came hurtling through the air from the jetty below. It exploded against the side of the half-track, blowing it sickeningly to the right. The tracks flailed across the dying boy's body shredding it to red pulp.

'Look out!' the Count screamed. '*LOOK OUT!*'

At full tilt the armoured snout rammed into the squat little WC.

Just before Otto's face slammed into the back of Cheetham's seat, he caught a crazy glimpse of a one-legged old boy in general's uniform, with his trousers down to reveal an exceedingly skinny rump. His final impression was a startled looking distinguished face flying through the air on the seat of a thunderbox to come slapping down on the deck of the waiting ferry. Behind him he heard the Count say faintly, 'Goodbye Benno. Have a nice trip,' then he passed out . . .

Things happened fast after that. One minute after Baron von Borkenheim had suffered his wound at last (though admittedly it was one he would never be able to exhibit in public, unfortunately) the engineer sergeant standing on the deck of the ferry steaming hastily out of the harbour, blew his charges. The jetty trembled like a live thing, with frantic little puffs of grey smoke erupting from the cracks which had suddenly appeared everywhere, before flying high in the air in a great spout of ugly red flame.

Five miles to the east, Brigadier Currie, a tall lean Lancers officer commanding a mixed force of tanks and commandos which had just landed up the coast in order to reach Messina before Patton, rose high in the turret of the lead Sherman and ignoring the few slugs coming his way from the remaining demoralized Italian snipers who had been abandoned by their comrades, cried, 'The Hun is doing a bunk, chaps!' He slapped his fly whisk against the steel turret as if he were back in the Lancers urging on some reluctant nag, 'Come on. Let's ride to the sound of the guns! *Driver advance!*' Ducking his head back into cover he kicked the shoulder of the driver somewhere down below in the glowing green gloom of the tank. 'Come on, old chap, let's get the jolly old digit out of the jolly old orifice. *The race is on!*'

To the west on the heights above Messina, the great spurt of flame coming from the docks had the same effect upon the Americans who had been spending a pleasant morning receiving the plump be-sashed civic dignitaries come to pay an official visit to the American HQ. Patton, who had just roared in and had taken in the scene with an angry glare, 'What in Sam Hill's name, are you guys sitting around here on your fat duffs for?' he bellowed above the roar of German guns now being fired across the straits of Messina from the mainland to cover the withdrawal of General von Borkenheim and his rear-guard, 'Get the hell down there and capture the city. And for Chrissake, make sure the Limeys don't capture the goddam place again after we've taken it. Oh hell,' he pushed aside the infantry divisional commander who was just in the middle of having his photograph taken with the Mayor of Messina (he had thought it would have made a nice souvenir for his wife in the States), 'I'll do it myself!' Agilely he bounded into his scout car. 'Okay, driver,' he yelled above the boom of the gunfire across the Straits, 'get the lead out of ya butt! *Let's go!*' He tugged hard at the cord which agitated the twin high-pitched klaxons.

Sirens screaming shrilly, the scout car lurched forward, scattering fat little Italians clad in dark frock-coats and striped pants on all sides, with General Patton standing rigidly upright in the turret wearing his Impatient Man-of-Action Number One Face. The last leg of the race for Messina had commenced.

*

Otto awoke with a groan to find his face nestling in what seemed to him a valley of warm pulsating flesh. He blinked hard several times and wished the next moment he hadn't. Some devil was busy thrusting red-hot skewers into the back of his head. His eyes came into focus and he saw that his head was resting between two of the most magnificent breasts he had ever seen. They were even bigger than those of Big-Lunged Rosi, a pavement-pounder friend of his mother's, who was so well-endowed that she had to enter buildings sideways and had once been accused by a somewhat timid customer of trying to 'breast' him to death, as she had galloped him around the mattress (indeed the little fellow had been heavily bruised around the face for weeks afterwards). 'God in heaven,' he exclaimed, pushing the Italian woman away and sitting up, 'where did you get so much wood in front of the door from?'

'*Como . . . como?*' the woman said in bewilderment, trying to stuff them back into her low-cut peasant blouse, as if she were putting melons into a too small bag.

'Forget it,' Otto growled and peered around him.

Al Cheetham, the alcohol obviously having hit him now, sprawled drunkenly over the shattered wheel of the half-track singing sotto-voce, '*Tight as a drum, never been done, Queen of All the Fairies, Isn't it a pity she's only got one titty to feed the baby on . . .*' He grinned at Otto inanely. The Count, surrounded by a group of admiring Sicilians, already well into his newly found role of 'American liberator' was giving an impassionate speech about democracy and the benefits of Big Business. Only Wipem seemed still interested in the war. Muttering furiously to himself, he was attempting to load one of the abandoned German 57mm cannon that were scattered everywhere above the shattered dock in order to return the fire coming from over the water.

Otto turned his attention back to the Count, who was now holding up a bottle of Coca Cola which he'd found somewhere in the jumbled mess at the back of the half-track and declaiming, 'Coca Cola – coke, we call it, citizens – is the symbol of our freedom-loving democracy. Some countries such as yours which don't have democracy do not understand the political message of this innocent little bottle of pleasant-tasting liquid—'

Otto could not listen to any more. He pushed his way through the crowd of impressed Sicilians and past a press cameraman who was taking the historic photograph of the Count holding up his bottle which would appear in the morning's edition of *Il Popolo* bearing the caption. '*Democracy Comes to Sicily in a Bottle! Courtesy the United States Army*' (Forty years later older Sicilians would remember that memorable photo with tears in their eyes). 'For shit's sake,' he growled, 'get off your shitting soapbox and let's make tracks while there's still shitting time!'

'Time, Otto,' the Count said pleasantly. 'We have all the time in the world. These poor people have been under foreign yoke for two thousand years, you know. The Greeks, the Romans, the Franks, the Arabs—'

'Fuck the Greeks – and the Arabs too!' Otto interrupted crudely. 'We've done what Patton and Colonel Mulligan wanted us to do. It's time for us to do a bunk, Count. The whole shitting place is falling apart.' With his free hand he indicated the confused mess of the harbour, fielding off the big-breasted Sicilian girl who was attempting to nestle his head among those mountains of flesh yet once again, a loving almost maternal look on her dark, pudding face. 'Get off!'

'But why, Otto, let us enjoy the fruits of the victory of our brave American boys.'

'Stop that gassing up there!' Wipem called angrily, madly swinging his cannon to the right, 'and come and help me!'

'What's the matter, Captain?' the Count called urgently, suddenly full of patriotic fervour once more.

'A goddamned enemy tank column – that's what's the

matter. Look!' Otto and the Count swung their gaze to the east.

The American Captain was right. Clouds of dust rolled ever closer, through which they could just catch a quick glimpse of dark steel monsters.

'They can't be ours,' Wipem panted, feverishly attempting to swing the cannon round to face the new danger. 'The US Seventh Army is coming in from the west. Now for God's sake give me a hand! Quick!'

Obediently the two friends pelted down the quay to help while, leaning drunkenly on the wheel, Cheetham trilled, '*The village idiot, he was there. And did his fav'rite trick. He pulled his foreskin over his head – and whistled down his prick.*'

Madly Otto and the Count heaved and shoved at the two metal trails forcing the ton and a half cannon round to face the tanks, which were rattling closer by the second, while Wipem pulled a gleaming shell free from inside the metal shield. Desperately he fumbled with the controls of the unfamiliar weapon until suddenly the breech snapped open to reveal a gaping hole. 'In there!' Otto gasped.

Wipem shoved in the shell. The breech lever clicked upwards automatically and slapped his arm painfully. 'Blast and damn!' he yelped through gritted teeth and squinted through the rubber-rimmed telescope. The dust was too thick for him to identify the lead tank. All he could see was that frighteningly impressive long cannon it bore. If he didn't open fire first, the thing would make hamburger-meat out of them. 'Watch out!' he yelled, 'I'm going to fire!'

The Count thrust his fingers into his ears and closed his eyes. Otto half-turned away.

The American jerked at the firing lever. The gun erupted in sudden fury. They had forgotten to apply the brakes and it sprang straight into the air to come thundering down with its right wheel on the Count's foot. Wipem was unfortunate too. As the cannon came shooting back, he was directly in front of the breech. It flew open in a cloud of acrid choking grey smoke. The used, steaming shell-case shot out and hit him right between the legs. He slammed to the ground five yards away, holding his testicles crying, as he writhed back and forth in pain, '*I'm ruined! For God's sake, I'm ruined for life!*'

At the wheel of the half-track, Cheetham sang happily, '*Big balls, small balls, balls as big as ya head, give 'em a twist about ya neck and throw 'em right over ya head.*'

Brigadier Currie's Sherman staggered suddenly, reared up in the air, and came to an abrupt stop, its right track sliding to the rear with an air of inevitability like a suddenly severed limb. He caught himself at the turret just in time, his nostrils suddenly assailed by the cloying stench of gunpowder and scorched metal. 'I say,' he said to no one in particular, 'they've gone and shot the damned nag from beneath, what!' He tut-tutted severely while below the driver vomited noisily and in the turret the gunner, an elderly corporal from Belfast with eighteen children and two common-law wives back in the Bogside, started to say the Act of Contrition at a cracking pace.

Behind the wrecked Sherman in the suddenly stalled column, Blackie Burrows flung up his binoculars and focused them on the lone gun outlined against the fires of the burning dockyard quite clearly. A dark saturnine face that seemed familiar leapt into view; then another one, broad, handsome and winning; and finally a third one, only too well remembered, fleshly handsome and dramatic, with a mop of uncombed white hair topping it. 'Good God, Carruthers,' he gasped as shaken as he had ever been in all his life, 'it's worse than the day we found old Jumbo Horrocks after the Pathans had stuck a stake up his—' He caught himself just in time and shuddered violently.

'What is it, sir?' Carruthers cried in alarm, as Brigadier Currie staggered from his stricken tank and began to stride down the column looking for another vehicle, while the commanders bent into their turrets trying to look as if their attention was elsewhere in the hope he wouldn't see them. 'In God's name,' he shrieked when his chief didn't answer, 'what did you just see, sir?'

'Them!' Blackie Burrows croaked, pointing a hand that shook violently in the direction of the harbour, not caring now that he was revealing his toothless gums. 'It's those swine who . . . who biffed me in the face . . . They've just had the audacity to . . . to fire on the Brig!'

At 10.30 precisely on the morning of August 17th, 1943 Patton's scout car with three outsize silver stars on its bonnet started to edge its way through the ruins of Messina towards what was left of city hall. The relieved citizens cheering the tall erect General in his faultlessly pressed gardines who stood there bearing his Benevolent Despot Sun King Look, waving regally to left and right, while saying out of the corner of his mouth to his bemused aide, 'My Seventh Army has done a better job on this place than the earthquake in 1909, eh[1] Codman?'

The vehicle swung round a corner. On both sides of the *piazza* heavily armed MPs had taken up their positions, their tommy-guns directed at the wildly cheering natives, jumping up and down in their excitement, with here and there girls flinging rose-petals down in front of the scout car. It came to a stop just as a dust-covered, agitated Brigadier Currie, riding on the top of a Sherman and followed by the rest of the British column came hurrying in from the eastern road. Patton didn't waste time. Swiftly he jumped down from the scout car and stood on the steps of the town hall, as if he had been waiting there a very long time, his face set in his Good-Natured Punctuality Is the Courtesy of Kings Look.

Currie swallowed hard and mumbled, 'Crumbs,' as he

[1] The Messina earthquake of that year killed 78,000 citizens

saw Patton; then he recovered, 'Driver halt!' he commanded and as the tank rumbled to a stop, sprang from it and advanced on a waiting Patton, trying to smile the best he could although he knew now his chances of getting a division under Monty were virtually nil. He snapped to attention and looked up at the American General, 'I congratulate you, sir. It was a jolly good race!'

The Italians broke out in spontaneous applause as if this little scene had been played especially to entertain them.

For a while the two Generals chatted, seemingly unaware of the thousands of cheering Italians on all sides, until Colonel Codman, Patton's personal aide, tugged his sleeve with unusual forwardness. 'Sir, an officer messenger has just delivered this.' He indicated the envelope marked *Top Secret, – Personal and Confidential* and initialled *DDW*. Patton frowned and excused himself, the Brigadier saluted and turned back to his own men, 'All right chaps,' he said, 'better start bulling up the vehicles or something for when General Montgomery arrives.'

Patton stared at the buff envelope. The initials were those of his chief Eisenhower, back in Africa. 'Any idea what's in it, Codman?' he asked.

Codman lied glibly, not daring to look Patton in the eye, 'No sir.'

Patton opened it with a quick rip and stared short-sightedly at the text, too vain to put on his glasses in public, especially on a great day like this when he had beaten Montgomery to Messina and ended the 36-day campaign in Sicily. His lips moving silently he began to read, his thin face growing more and more sombre by the second. 'I am well aware,' Eisenhower had written, 'of the necessity for tough ruthlessness on the battlefield. I clearly understand that firm and drastic measures are at times necessary in order to secure desired objectives. But this does not excuse brutality, abuse of the sick, nor exhibition of uncontrollable temper in front of subordinates. If there is any element of truth in the allegations accompanying this letter, I must so seriously question your good judgement and self-discipline as to raise serious doubts in my mind as to your future usefulness . . .'

Patton could read no more. He lowered the letter, almost dropping it from his suddenly nerveless fingers, face pale with shock, eyes blurred.

'Bad news, sir?' Codman asked softly.

Patton didn't seem to hear. Two grey tears started to trickle down his skinny cheeks slowly, and for the first time since he had known him, Codman realized just what a very old man General Patton was. 'I'm all washed up, Codman,' Patton said in a thick whisper. 'Washed up.' Without another word, he turned and began to trail wearily to the waiting scout car. He didn't look back.

'There they are!' It was not the words, but the tone of that hard upper-class British voice which alerted Otto and the Count to their danger, as they hurried through the thronged streets. The exuberant Sicilians who were now beginning to get drunk under the dour gaze of the bone-weary GIs squatting in the gutters everywhere, as if they were the victors and the dirty, unshaven, morose Americans were the losers.

Instinctively Otto grabbed the Count's arm and hissed, 'Come on, let's run!'

'But what—'

Otto didn't give him time to ask his question. Instead he forced him forward and together they began to hustle their way through the mad throng. Behind them whistles shrilled. There was the sound of heavy feet running. A swarthy-faced Italian tried to bar Otto's way. His fist lashed out and the man went reeling back, clutching a big nose from which bright blood squirted. The two of them raced round a corner. To their left there was one of those typical, ornate Sicilian churches, to the right a café. Otto's heart sank, for the little cobbled street ended in a blank wall, too high for the Count to scale! He made a quick decision. 'Into the church,' he gasped. 'There'll be more than one—'

He never finished. The heavy, brass-shod butt of an Army rifle slammed into the back of his skull and he pitched face-forward into the dirty, overflowing gutter. A red mist threatened to overcome him, but just before it did, he heard a harsh official voice ask in English, 'And what are the charges, sir?' The upper-class voice which had first alerted him to his danger answered, 'Oh, for a start Sergeant, espionage, firing upon British troops . . .'

Otto decided he had had enough. He let the red mist swamp him and passed out.

Standing next to Blackie Burrows, his hands already cruelly handcuffed, the Count nodded his approval sadly and said in German, 'Yes, poor Otto my friend, it is better to die thus than languish in a cell for a lifetime . . .'

PART THREE: ESCAPE TO BATTLE

'Onward conscript soldiers, marching as to war! You'd all be dead men now, if you'd volunteered before.' *WWI ditty sung to the tune of ONWARD CHRISTIAN SOLDIERS*

ONE

Now the war had passed Sicily. It had gone across the Straits of Messina on to the mainland and already Allied troops were pressing up the boot of Italy. The fascists had deposed Mussolini and the one-time dictator had been kidnapped by his own police and transported to some unknown hiding place. Then they had sued for peace. But they had been too slow about doing so and by the time they had, the Germans had been in charge of most key points in the North at least and were feverishly seeking the missing Mussolini so that they could place him at the head of a new fascist state and rally some Italians at least to the German cause.

Far across the Atlantic, the 'Patton slapping incident', as it was now called, had created a scandal that had shaken America from coast to coast. Congress had called for an inquiry and General Eisenhower, always frightened of adverse press publicity no longer attempted to protect his old friend. Besides the Secretary of State for War Stimson was determined to punish Patton and he was too powerful a person to fight. Eisenhower's request that Patton should be given command of the US Fifth Army in Italy was turned down brusquely. So 'Blood an' Guts' had been left to brood and stew in his own juice in his gilded cage in Palermo, the former royal palace, without an active command, his only role to fool the Germans that the Allies might be planning an attack on what Churchill called the 'soft underbelly of Europe', the Balkans.

And the prisoners of the 'Palermo Central Cage', as the largest Allied holding prison on the island was called, would often see him riding his white horse morosely accompanied by only a single aide, a beaten man who never even looked up when some bold prisoner called down a crude remark from his cell. Even the old taunt – 'Who ya gonna slap today, General?' – seemed to have no effect on him. He expressed his mood that autumn to Codman, his loyal aide, more than once, 'Charley, I feel lower than a whale's ass!'

'Poor General,' the Count said sadly one afternoon in early September as he watched Patton guiding his white charger through the rocks that littered the barren country outside the sprawling 18th century prison, 'how sad he looks. It must be torture for him imprisoned alone in that great gloomy palace – without anything to do and no one wanting to know him now that he's in disgrace.' The Count shook his white head miserably. 'What a tragedy, what a tragedy indeed,' he said, as the General and Codman passed from sight.

Otto, clad in the loose ill-fitting denim suit of the military prison, with a large white 'P' for 'prisoner' painted on the back and a neat little white heart on the front ('so the sentry doesn't have to bother to take aim when he plugs yer through it,' as one of the military policeman guards had explained crudely), looked up from where he was crouched against the grey dirty stone wall of the cell, covered with the graffiti of two centuries of doomed men. 'Hm,' he grunted miserably, 'hard luck on him. Down to his last horse and only getting four square meals a day, probably limited to a mere eight courses, while we're feasting our faces on – *that!*' He indicated the piece of stale hard-tack, which, together with a cup of weak cocoa, had been their 'tea' and was now being used as bait by a group of prisoners to entice the evil-looking black cockroaches from their hiding places to start on the daily 'Beetle Derby'.

The Count beamed down at his old friend encouragingly. 'Don't take it to heart, Otto, my boy. All will come out in the wash in the end. I'm sure that when Captain Wipem and Lieutenant Cheetham find out what has happened to us they will do their utmost to right this wrong. And those fellers,' he indicated the other prisoners with a dramatic sweep of a hand, now covered with red bug bites, 'might appear to be a rough sort of bunch, but you must admit they are the salt of the earth.'

Otto looked at their companions in the big, high-ceilinged cell. They were all types and colours from a dozen Allied nations; Australians, New Zealanders, Indians, plenty of Tommies of course, even a fiery-haired Scot in a kilt, who slept with it pinned between his naked buttocks at night for obvious reasons. 'Salt of the earth!' he grunted sourly,' a bunch of pimps, deserters, black-marketeers, pox-merchants—' the rest of his miserable litany was drowned by an excited cry of '*they're off!*' and even the Scotsman forgetting his secret in the excitement as the black beetles, urged on by the tipsters with gentle prods from pieces of straw, started to crawl across the floor, bent down revealing an ample portion of naked buttocks.

Otto groaned and closed his eyes; if he saw another 'Beetle Derby' he would scream out loud. The way the bored prisoners fawned over their pet cockroaches nauseated him, just as everything else in the 'Palermo Central Cage' did. Sometimes he even wished that the Tommies would hurry with their trial and get it over with, whatever the damn outcome. But he knew that could not be. The prison was filled to overflowing with military criminals of all kinds, ranging from black marketeers and deserters to rapists and murderers. The authorities would take months to clear up the backlog and every day brought new prisoners from Italy, the 'Free English' as they called themselves quite cheerfully, men who had simply walked away from some front-line unit or other and taken to the hills where 'I found myself an Eyetie bint and a Mamma', as they always explained, 'the one to give me a bit o' the other in kipp and Mamma to cook the egg and chips. Lovely grub, mate. Nowt beats getting yer feet under the table, specially if it's an Eyetie one.'

The Count walked over to watch the race, while Otto

listened half-heartedly to the prisoner they called 'the Sailor' – he had deserted to the Italians in 1940 and had been found by the Americans when they had captured Palermo three years later – telling one of his tales of his long service with 'Royal'. 'The Chinks,' he was saying in a broad Devonshire accent, 'think live monkey is a real delicacy, you see. So they wedge a little chimp below a table with only its poor old head popping through a hole in the centre while all the customers wait with their spoons at the ready, all jabbering away in chink, black eyes popping out of their yellow mugs with excitement. Then the cook – if you can call him that – takes a little chopper and before you can say Jack Robinson has whipped off the top of the poor beast's skull.' He paused for effect and Otto listened sickened but curious, 'Then what do you think the Chinks do, mates? I'll tell yer. They dip their tools inside the chimp's noddle and start eating its brains. That's what they do, the filthy heathen buggers.' Even the hard-boiled prisoners were appalled and someone said in a thick voice. 'Go on, Sailor, yer having us on. Pull the other bleeding leg it's got bells on it!'

The Sailor wasn't put out. 'It's the God-honest truth, mate. I'm telling yer. All these wogs have funny eating habits. Did yer know for instance, that these here Sicilians eat cats and when there are no moggies about, they catch the poor little sparrers from the trees and nosh them too!'

'No wonder they all look like they do,' someone said, 'eating moggies and dickie birds. What kind of grub is that? You give me something solid and British like stewed eels or . . . er . . . tripe and onions or pigs' trotters any day.'

'Aw knock it off, Sailor,' a harsh nasal voice snarled in an almost perfect American accent. 'What do you limeys know about chow anyway? Stewed tea and corned beef fritters is the best you can produce!'

Otto did not need to look up to know who the speaker was. It was 'the Soldier', Toni Pacino, a swarthy-skinned, pock-marked runt of an Italian-American who boasted that he had once been a 'soldier' for the Mafia in the States before he had been sent to St Quentin, from whence he had been released at the request of Lucky Luciano in order to make contact with the local Mafia in Sicily and so help the American landings. For some reason about which he was not prepared to talk, unlike most of his fellow prisoners, he, too, had landed in the 'Palermo Central Cage'.

The Sailor laughed easily. 'Go on, Soldier, stick yer own cock up yer behind and give yersen a cheap thrill.'

The others laughed too and Otto looked up to see the Italian-American's swarthy face flush a dusky angry red, his black eyes glittering dangerously as he broke away from the crowd listening to the Sailor and pushed his way to the window, clenched fists dug deep into his fatigue trousers' pockets. Otto frowned thinking the open-faced, blue-eyed old sailor better watch himself. He wouldn't be surprised if the Soldier had a knife concealed about him somewhere, nor if he used it when he thought it opportune to do so.

He dismissed both the Sailor and the Soldier, and concentrated on his own problems, while the men urged their beetles on excitedly at the far end of the big cell.

After the first shock of their arrest had worn off, Otto's mood had alternated between resignation and a desire to get away from the Cage before it was too late. Unlike the Count, who rarely despaired and was always convinced there was a silver lining on the horizon somewhere sooner or later, he did not think that they would be saved by Wipem and Cheetham. He reasoned that they had gone to the mainland with the rest of the American troops, where the war would have swallowed them up again, their two erstwhile comrades Otto and the Count long-forgotten. For all he knew they might well be dead, especially Wipem who was always taking impossible risks. No, he told himself once again, as he crouched there in the noisy cell, no one would help them. They would have to help themselves.

During their daily hourly exercise period, he had had plenty of time to study the ancient prison with its crumbling stucco walls and the temporary wooden towers, which the English had built and manned with machine-gunners as soon as they had taken the place over. He had come to the conclusion it was not that very formidable. The walls were full of holes and although they were high it wouldn't be too difficult to scale them. Nor were the wooden guard towers that great an obstacle. Due to the construction of the place there was plenty of dead ground at night where an escaper could conceal himself in the shadows. Even the gunners presented a minimal risk for they often went to sleep during the long hours of the night vigil, agreeing with one of their number to stay awake just in case an officer unexpectedly made his rounds. He knew from his own observations through the cell window that by three o'clock most of the guards were fast asleep.

There was one problem, however, an insurmountable one, or so it seemed to him: that of his fellow prisoners. Even if he managed to pick the ancient lock of their cell or overpower a careless guard bringing in their rations, he couldn't rely on the others to keep quiet. One or the other would raise the alarm before he and the Count had reached the end of the cell corridor, he knew that implicitly. One would do it for reward, extra rations, cigarettes, chocolate; another because he felt that an escape would endanger him in his attempt to stay in the safety of the Cage, and lay him open once again to the horror and dangers of the front.

Otto sitting there in the gathering darkness, while the Beetle Derby ran its course, bit his bottom lip; there seemed no way round that particular, overwhelming problem. As always, man was his own worse enemy . . .

Two days later, as he and the Count circled the yard in single file to the tune of the usual mocking song sung by the Sailor, '*Ring-a-ring a roses, pocket full of posies*,' Corporal Chalmers, one of the hard-faced MPs watching the prisoners, called, 'Hey you two Jerries, over here! You're wanted.'

Otto and the Count stopped in their tracks and the Sailor simpered in a shrill falsetto as he trudged past Otto, 'Give the nice corporal a kissie from me, won't yer darling?' He blew the red-faced MP a wet kiss, as the two comrades turned and set off in the NCO's direction.

'Follow me,' he snapped, obviously glad to get away from the Sailor, 'smartly now. You've got a visitor. Left, right, left right, swing them arms! Bags o' swank! Remember who you are now!'

Otto groaned but followed the Corporal's commands obediently and marched smartly behind the Count, who was swinging his arms level with his shoulders, as if he were a guardsman on sentry outside Buckingham Palace. They marched into the main building boots echoing hollowly on the flagged corridor.

'Mark time!' Corporal Chalmers barked, twisting his head to one side, his face suddenly purple, as if he was in the last throes of acute apoplexy. 'Come on now, you two, get them knees up, right up! Don't worry nothing'll fall out. And if it does, I'll pick it up for yer. Left, right!'

Wearily Otto did as he was ordered, knowing the Corporal was only putting on this show because the camp commandant's office was two doors up, wondering too who their visitor could be.

'Halt!' Chalmers commanded.

They brought their right feet down loudly on the stone floor and waited for the command to stand at ease.

The command came not from Chalmers in the form of a harsh, hysterical bark, but from within the office, the door of which had just opened, spoken in a familiar soft southern drawl, 'Okay, at ease, guys.'

They spun round as one, faces suddenly animated with new hope. It was Lt Al Cheetham all right, a weary grin on his bronzed face, now a lot thinner than when they had last seen it, his right arm clutched in a dirty sling held tightly to his shabby civilian jacket that appeared much too short for him. 'Friar Tuck!' the Count gasped. 'I knew you wouldn't let us down.'

Cheetham frowned and said, 'Gino Paolo to be exact. My new cover name, but no matter.'

'Will you be wanting me, sir?' Chalmers asked, emphasizing the 'sir', as if he weren't quite sure whether the shabby civilian deserved the address. 'They're reputed to be dangerous.'

Cheetham shook his head. 'No, I think I can handle them. It's a security matter, I'd like to talk to them privately.'

'As you wish, sir. But I'll have to leave the door open and watch you from there, sir. Camp Commandant's instructions, sir.'

Cheetham waved his uninjured arm at the Corporal. 'Sure . . . sure, no sweat. Can I give 'em a pack of cigarettes each?' Hastily he added, 'And why not have a pack yourself? I'm sure you wouldn't mind a decent American smoke after that Egyptian camel crap they give you boys.'

Chalmers beamed. 'Yes sir, it's all right, I think. Thank you, sir, don't mind if I do. Those V-Cigarettes we get on ration are a bit hard on the old tonsils.'

Beaming madly Cheetham led the old comrades into the room, placing them on two wooden chairs which seemed to be the place's only furniture, standing looking down at them with his back to the door and Corporal Chalmers, now busy ripping open the gift.

'And how is Captain Wipem?' the Count asked, about to do the same as Chalmers until he saw that Cheetham was frowning severely at the cigarettes he held in his hand, shaking his head slightly as he did so.

'Dead,' he answered. 'We got caught in a Kraut ambush twenty kilometres north of Bari. He was dead before he hit the ground.' He sniffed. 'I won't be hypocritical about it – it wasn't a particularly great loss to the world. Put the smokes away for later, Otto,' he hissed urgently. 'Yes,' he continued, his voice normal again. 'It's this damned business with Mussolini. The Limeys are looking for him, we're looking for him, and of course the Krauts are looking for him. The guy might have lost all his power but he'd be a damn useful figurehead for the Krauts. That's why we're so damn anxious to find him before they do.'

Otto absorbed the information for a moment before nodding at Cheetham's bandaged arm and asking, 'Did you run into trouble too?'

'Yeah, kinda. It was the same ambush. One of the Krauts let me and the wops I was with have a burst at fifty yards range. The wops were all killed. I just got winged.' He winked solemnly at Otto, who stared at him in bewilderment. 'Remind me to let me show you the wound before I go, won't ya?'

'Yes, of course,' Otto stuttered, wondering what the big American was up to.

The amused look vanished from Cheetham's face and the Count could now see just how worn he was; he had aged a lot since they had last seen him and there was something about his eyes that suggested he was no longer the innocent optimistic American he once was. 'I even managed to get to General Patton to talk to him about you fellows,' he continued. 'I told him that everything you did, you did on orders and the British have got the wrong end of the stick. But,' he shrugged, 'Patton is no longer in a position to do anything for you. He's all washed up – just as I am.'

'You mean the charges stand?' Otto said quietly.

Cheetham nodded morosely. 'Yeah, you'll have to stand trial without any help from us. Uncle Sam is a hard master. He doesn't always reward his obedient servants, I'm afraid.' He hesitated and looked hard at both of them in turn. 'There's no question about it, you two will have to help yourselves, savvy.'

Otto's heart suddenly started to beat faster. This was no casual visit. Cheetham had something in mind for them. The packs of cigarettes and his arm had something to do with it, though he didn't know how. 'You say, you're all washed-up, Friar,' he said urgently, trying to keep the conversation going so that Chalmers enjoying the rich flavour of the American cigarette in the doorway should not get suspicious. 'Why? What happened?'

'Oh, nothing much. I guess a year of combat is about enough for any guy. I've requested a transfer back to the ZI and Washington has approved.[1] I'm going back as an instructor to one of the new OSS outfits they're setting up for the Pacific.' He sighed, 'I guess I'm getting sick of Europe, though as a kid I would have given my eye-teeth to have gotten here.'

'Sick of Europe?' the Count objected, obviously still unaware that there was any real significance behind Cheetham's visit. 'How can anyone ever get sick of Europe?'

Cheetham smiled wanly at him. 'It's easy, Count,' he said. 'Just find a bunch of wop kids in uniform all under eighteen, their hands tied behind their backs with wires and a nice neat bullet hole at the back of their heads. It can make you go off the place real quick.' He shrugged. 'Anyone could have shot them, I'll admit. The British, the Americans, the Germans, perhaps even their own people. But that doesn't matter. What *does* matter is that that sort of thing is happening in Europe today and has been for the last three and half years. So—' he broke off suddenly and grinned ruefully at them. 'Al Cheetham just stepped down from his soapbox. Otto, would you like to see my wound before I take off?'

Bewildered by the request as well as Cheetham's sudden change of mood, Otto heard himself say, 'yes'. He rose to his feet as Cheetham held up his bandaged arm stiffly, as if it were very sore.

At the door Chalmers took another deep drag at his cigarette. He didn't seem interested.

'There,' Cheetham said, holding the arm right under Otto's nose. 'Nasty looking scratch, aint' it? . . . *Quick, rip it off!*' he hissed urgently.

In one and the same moment, Otto reached inside the

[1] Zone of the Interior – military jargon for the USA

sling and ripped the little black object tied there by plaster from Cheetham's bare arm.

'Ouch,' he said and grinned at Otto, sudden tears in his eyes, whether from pain or emotion, Otto would never find out for Al Cheetham never would reach the ZI. The *Luftwaffe* saw to that. He reached out his good hand. 'Well, Otto, all the best,' he said, raising his voice for Chalmers' benefit, 'look after yourself, kid. I'll keep my fingers crossed for you. Perhaps we'll meet again after the war.' He smiled at Otto, but his eyes no longer lit up as they had once done.

'Count, try to keep your nose clean and don't let your imagination run away with you, if you get my meaning.' He winked at the older man, who as always on such occasions was moved, tears gleaming suddenly in his eyes.

He shook Cheetham's hand fervently. 'Thank you, my boy. God go with you . . . and don't lose your faith in poor old sordid Europe altogether, *please!*'

'I'll try to make a point of it, Count,' Cheetham said easily, turning to the Corporal. 'All right, the rogues are yours again. Wheel 'em out.'

'Sir!' Chalmers dropped his cigarette and ground it out neatly on the floor. 'All right, you two,' he barked, 'let's be having yer! At the double now . . . left, right . . . left right! Bags o' swank now, *swing them arms!*'

Lieutenant Cheetham sighed, as the sound of their heavy nailed boots echoed down the tight stone confines of the corridor. Outside in the exercise yard someone was singing in a soft southern voice the sad little hit of that autumn, '*Spring is gonna be a little late this year*', and from the sea a breeze had sprung up, chasing the brown autumnal leaves that lay everywhere on the stone. Suddenly the view was as sombre as his mood. Lieutenant Cheetham let his shoulders sink as if in defeat. Slowly he turned and began to walk down the corridor, out into the sunshine which no longer warmed . . .

TWO

'Well?' Otto asked urgently, as the two comrades crouched around the evil-smelling 'piss-bucket' in the dark corner of the big cell; it was the only place in their prison avoided by the others – no amount of lime could kill its repulsive stench. 'What's in yours?'

The Count threw a furtive look at their fellow prisoners. No one was looking in their direction, for already they were beginning to hunt for suitable cockroaches for the evening's 'Beetle Derby'. Even the Sailor was busy searching, his tall tales about his days in the pre-war Royal Navy forgotten for the moment. 'Money,' he whispered. 'Italian and American.'

'How much?'

'A hundred dollars and three thousand lira.'

'Good old Cheetham!' Otto breathed. 'And I bet that didn't come out of OSS funds, but out of his own pocket.'

'And you – what was in your pack, Otto?'

Otto turned his back to the others and flashed open his right hand. In its centre lay a small silver key. 'This!' he said excitedly.

'It's not to the cell-door, Otto, is it?' the Count asked puzzled.

'Of course not, you silly old fart!' Otto snapped. 'It's the ignition key to a boat.'

'*A boat!*'

'For Chrissake!' Otto hissed. 'Keep it down, will yer? You don't want everyone to know, do you?'

'Sorry, Otto,' the Count said crestfallen, looking round the cell quickly. But the others were still occupied with their beetle-hunt. Only the runtish soldier, the Italian-American, was not participating. He squatted with his back to the dirty stone, cleaning the filth from underneath his overlong nails with what appeared to be a piece of wire. 'A boat?'

'Yes. It's written here on the inside of the pack. "*OSS launch anchored to the right of hamlet St Maria, four kilometres east of Messina. Guarded by Carbinieri in OSS pay. No problem. Gassed up and ready to go. Good luck. AC. PS. Regards to the Führer when you see him.*" '

The Count's eyes gleamed. 'Oh, I say, Otto, how absolutely wonderful! A boat! The only way to get away from Sicily.' His face fell again, his enthusiasm vanished as quickly as it had come. 'But we've still got to get out of this hideous place,' he indicated the cell with a wave of his hand. 'Haven't we, Otto?'

'Yes,' Otto agreed, his face grim. 'But Cheetham did give me something else,' he added slowly.

'You mean when he asked you to look at his wound?'

Otto nodded.

'What was it?'

Otto put the key away again and tugged open the front of his denim blouse. There, resting between his shirt and belted trousers, was a small dark ugly object.

The Count caught his breath, his eyes widening. 'A pistol!' he gasped.

'A pistol,' Otto echoed. 'I suppose in the end that's the only damn key we can use.'

That night the two comrades huddled as far away from the others as possible as they tried to find a solution to the problem of escaping without the knowledge of their cell-mates; for some, they knew, would not hesitate to betray them.

For a while their discussion revolved around using the tiny pistol as a means of cowing the others into silence. But in the end Otto rejected the idea. 'Yes,' he had whispered, his mouth close to the Count's ear as they lay there on the dirty straw pallets, listening to the snores and groans of the sleeping men. 'For a while I think it'd do the trick. But once we were outside and couldn't use it on them, they'd be yelling their heads off for the guards and that would be that.'

As outside the ancient citadel clock chimed midnight with grave metallic solemnity, the first vague plan began to emerge, as the Count suggested. 'Then if we can't leave them behind, Otto, we must take them with us.'

Otto considered the proposal for an instant and said, 'You mean the whole miserable bunch?'

'Yes. Some will be willing to go. The Sailor and the Soldier for example. They have everything to gain from escaping – I'm sure that Soldier is here for murder, he looks the part, I must say – and everything to lose by staying in here. The others we will simply force to come with us, whether they like it or not.'

'A mass escape?' Otto mused, rubbing his unshaven chin thoughtfully, while down at the far end of the dark cell someone cried out in his sleep, torn perhaps by the nightmare of a battle past. 'You can do what yer like, Sarnt-Major, I'm not going up the line agen. I've had it, I tell yer! Had it fer fucking good! It'll be tricky, Count, trying to keep control of those bastards. I don't trust one of them.'

'Agreed, Otto. I share your feelings. But we can use those who want to go to keep those who don't under control.'

'Of course,' Otto conceded. 'Then the trouble is – what to do with them when we've got them outside? Unless—' he stopped short.

'Unless what, Otto?'

'Unless we blow the whistle on the bastards once we're out and let the authorities get all confused trying to round them up. Most of the rats haven't deserved anything better. They'd sell their own grandmother, so for a change they'd be the ones to be sold.'

The Count considered for a moment and then said, 'All right, Otto, let's start planning it that way. The question is who should we pick first to take into our confidence, or rather,' he grinned wanly in the light of the searchlight as it swept by the cell window and illuminated that grim place momentarily, '*part* of our confidence, I should say?'

Otto did not have to think long. 'First the Sailor, at least he's an honest rogue and then,' he frowned slightly, 'and then the Soldier. I don't trust him, but he's vicious and tough. The others are scared of him. What do you think, Count?'

The older man nodded. 'My choice exactly, Otto, and once they're in the picture we'd better keep our eyes on them, night and day, don't you agree?'

'Agreed.' Otto yawned. In five hours' time the heavy-booted guards would be coming marching down the corridor, banging on the doors of the cells with their pick handles, yelling their usual dawn litany of 'All right, you shower, hands off yer cocks and on with yer socks! Come on, wakey-wakey, let's be having you!' It was time for sleep. 'All right, Count, let's call it a day. Good night, Count.'

'Good night, Otto.'

They both lay back. Within minutes the Count was snoring softly at Otto's side, but somehow, tired as he was, Otto couldn't sleep. Instead he lay there on his back, hands under his head, trying to penetrate the darkness above him, his thoughts gloomy and depressing. In the end he fell into a troubled sleep, heavy with the knowledge that things would never be right again. Never . . .

'Cor, stone the ferking crows!' the Sailor said out of the corner of his mouth as they did their usual circle of the courtyard, shivering a little in the bitter wind that came from the sea and sent the dust whirling in mad little dances about their shuffling feet. 'Escape, now that really is a turn up for the ferking books! Better even than the morning after the night before in Port Said when I woke up with a brown bint in both arms—'

'Are you on?' Otto interrupted him firmly. 'Yes or no?'

' 'Course I'm on, mate,' the Sailor answered enthusiastically, in no way offended. 'When the Royal gets through trying me I'll be in the nick at Pompey for the rest of me born days. *You betcha I'm on!*'

The little Italian-American was not so hasty nor enthusiastic. In the centre of the room, the evening's Beetle Derby was reaching a noisy excited climax and while Count von der Weide kept a watchful eye on his cell-mates grouped there, Otto squatted at the wall next to the Soldier, telling him of their plan. At the first mention of escape, his eyes had gleamed excitedly, but only for a moment; thereafter they had resumed their old cold wary unblinking stare until Otto was finished. 'Well?' he asked.

The Soldier was not to be rushed. He took his time and Otto could see he was thinking hard; he imagined he could almost hear the little cogs clicking into place inside his skull as he calculated the gains and risks of the escape plan. Finally he spoke. 'Okay, so you wanna escape. Big deal!' he sneered, contorting his swarthy, pock-marked face. 'How ya gonna do it? Where's your artillery, brother?'

Otto was annoyed. The man got under his skin. He pulled aside his blouse to reveal the little pistol nestling in his belt.

'There!' he snapped angrily.

The Soldier whistled softly. 'So you've got a cannon, eh! Well, that sure is a start. But it ain't everything. Let me put the problems to ya, brother. One,' he ticked off the number on his nicotine-stained forefinger, 'somehow you've got to get through that door there. Two, across the courtyard without the bulls seeing ya. Three, up the wall, though I guess it ain't too difficult to get up. Four, and brother this is the sixty-four-dollar question, where ya going once you get outa the pen?' He stopped and waited with feigned patience as Otto prepared to answer his questions.

'One, we'll pick the lock. I've done it before and I don't think it will be too difficult, Soldier.'

The Italian-American nodded, as if he agreed, but remained silent.

'Two, we go out at three in the morning, taking *everybody* with us whether they want to go or not.' He tapped the butt of the pistol underneath his fatigue blouse. 'With this little friend in my hand, I don't think they're going to give me too much trouble.'

'Go on,' the Soldier prompted, obviously interested now.

'Three, I've studied the wall well enough during the exercise periods. It's full of footholds. I don't think it'll be too difficult to scale, even for the older people. They'll make it, they'll have to. I'll see to that.' He stopped.

In the centre of the room, the excited prisoners were pounding on the floor with their fists and blowing hard, heads close to the ground, in order to hurry their favourites to the 'winning post'.

'And four?' the Soldier persisted.

Otto thought fast. The less the Italian-American knew about the full plan, the better. 'I haven't gone into that one yet. I've been concentrating too much on the scheme to get out. First things first. Well, are you with us or aren't you?' he added, his voice harsh and threatening.

The Soldier was not impressed. 'First things first,' he said thoughtfully. 'Yeah, I guess you're right. Okay, I'm with you.' He bent his dark-haired greasy head for a moment so that Otto would not see the look in his eyes, then after a moment he raised it again and snapped, 'When?'

Otto hesitated for a moment only, then he said, 'Tomorrow night, and,' he added lowering his voice menacingly, 'if you've got any fancy ideas about betraying us, forget them. You won't live to realize them.'

Again the Soldier wasn't impressed. 'Don't piss your pants, Kraut, I won't betray you. I want out as much as anybody, 'cos I've got business to do out there, *important* business . . .'

THREE

All was silent save for the howl of the wind outside. To a tense, nervous Otto it seemed there might be a storm soon. The jail slept. The corridor outside was heavy with the sound of snores coming from the other cells. Crouched as he was at the door, he turned and nodded to the Soldier and the Sailor, both of whom had armed themselves with primitive clubs – legs from the cell's stools with a nail driven through them – to threaten the waverers. They nodded back that they were ready.

Carefully Otto inserted the long piece of wire into the big rusty lock, feeding it inside inch by inch, letting its malleable metal take on the shape of the interior. It scraped against the other end. Otto said a silent prayer, and turned. There was a slow click as the lock snapped open. He breathed out a sigh of relief. Holding his finger to his lips for silence, he indicated the Count, who was now armed with their pistol, to cover him.

He grasped the big handle and pulled. The door started to open with a rusty moan that seemed so loud to Otto that it had to wake everyone in the Cage. His heart beating furiously, he peered into the dimly-lit corridor, half expecting it to be filled with enraged guards. It was empty, save for a lone rat which scurried hastily for cover when it saw Otto. 'All right,' he whispered, 'follow me – in twos. And stick to the walls.'

As they had planned, Sailor's group took the left wall and the Soldier's the right, with Sailor and Soldier bringing up the rear just in case someone attempted to sneak off, while the Count, armed with his pistol, followed directly behind Otto, providing the kind of life insurance that Otto thought he needed against the bunch of rogues following him.

Now they began to creep along the shadows cast by the grey dripping walls, ducking as they passed each cell door just in case any of the inmates took it into his head to peer out of the little barred window. Otto came to the door at the end of the corridor, lit by two dull lamps, for although the war had long passed Sicily by, the authorities still observed the blackout regulations. Again he inserted his home-made skeleton key and again it worked without difficulty. Carefully he opened the door and turned left, hearing the wind grow louder now so that he knew he was heading for the open and the right direction.

Placing their feet down with elaborate care, the escapers began to make their way down the corridor which led to the outside, Otto in the lead already aware of the smell of fried sausage and egg coming from the right side of the passage further up. He frowned. That could indicate that not all the guards were asleep. Someone had got up and fried himself an early morning snack; sausage and egg were delicacies reserved for the guards in the Palermo Central Cage. He paused for a moment and turning to the others crouched tensely in the half darkness, pulled down the side of his right eye: the signal for extreme care. They nodded their understanding.

On tip-toe Otto continued, feeling slightly nauseated on an empty stomach at the smell, his nerves jingling like electric wires. He came level with the door from which the smell came. Fortunately it was closed, but it had an opaque glass panel. His heart almost stopped beating. Silhouetted perfectly through it, he could see a man standing up, mug in one hand, pistol outlined against his hip. He ducked hastily. The armed man inside had only to turn and he would have seen Otto there. His legs feeling like soft rubber, he stalked on, hoping against hope that all of the prisoners would keep their heads down below that glass panel and that no one would decide that this would be the moment to cry alarm. But none of them did. Two minutes later they were grouped tightly around the door leading to the courtyard. Noiselessly, Otto counted three to himself, took a deep breath and turned the handle. As he had hoped, it wasn't locked and for once someone had oiled the hinges. It opened without a sound.

He turned quickly and whispered out of the side of his mouth to the Count, 'Now stick to me like chewing gum, Count, when we get to the wall, you go first. I'll bunk you up. Clear?'

'Clear, Otto,' the Count answered in a frightened voice. For once he was not enjoying an 'adventure' as he was wont to call the desperate scrapes he was always getting Otto into. 'All right, here we go!'

Just as he turned, he caught one quick glimpse of the Soldier's dark malevolent eyes watching him intently. Somehow that intent gaze scared him more than what was to come. Then he dismissed the look and concentrated on the task ahead.

Outside all was darkness, with the shrubs that bordered the crumbling walls moving back and forth noiselessly, as the wind grew in intensity and the first heavy slow spots of rain came pattering down. Otto told himself that it was all to the good. A rainstorm would cover any noise they made and make the guards less watchful. 'All right, split up as agreed. Let's go! The Count and me will take the centre.'

Now the men, reluctant or willing, needed no urging. If the searchlight spotted them in the open courtyard, the men at the machine-guns would not hesitate to open fire. They'd be sitting ducks. Hastily the Sailor's and the Soldier's parties came streaming out of the door, splitting into two groups as agreed, while Otto and the Count doubled straight to the front.

The wind howled even more. The raindrops increased. The bushes swayed back and forth, whipped by the force of the storm to come. The Count ran with all his strength.

Even with the noise of the storm approaching, Otto could hear his harsh breathing and hoped the old man wouldn't have a heart attack with the strain. He flung hasty glances to left and right. Dark shapes were pelting for the wall everywhere. Sailor and Soldier had done their work well. None of their groups were lagging behind. On impulse he dug his hand into his pocket which contained the home-made flare, the boot polish handed out to the prisoners liberally by the guards, a bit of flannel and some melted candle wax. Once he and the Count were safe on the other side of the wall, he'd light it and fling it at the nearest guard tower. It should do the job of alarming the prison. While he and the Count made their escape, he reasoned that the waverers would be so frightened by the sudden light and resultant alarm that they would start surrendering. That should keep the guards off their backs until they reached the boat. He ran on.

A minute later they had reached the crumbling wall, in this spot set in the shadow cast by the nearest tower. 'God in heaven!' the Count gasped, the breath coming from his lungs as if from a broken leather bellows. 'I . . . really am too . . . old for this sort of thing, Otto!'

'Look at it as a kind of an adventure,' Otto hissed a little maliciously, wiping the raindrops from his face. 'I mean, don't you think it fun to be running around in the middle of the night in a rainstorm with a good chance of having yer turnip blown off if yer're a bit careless?'

'Please spare me the cynicism, Otto,' the Count quavered fearfully, flinging a frightened glance at the nearest tower, which was fortunately silent, its occupants obviously fast asleep secure in the thought that nobody would want to escape in this kind of weather.

'Yer,' Otto agreed, 'let's get on with it!' He bent down and cupped his hands, legs braced to take the strain. 'Hop up here and get cracking. I'll give you sixty seconds start, then I'm coming after yer. Once yer on top, wait for me and keep low so that yer silhouette don't give yer – Christ,' he groaned suddenly as he felt the Count's weight, 'what've you been eating?'

The Count didn't answer; he was too afraid to speak. Hesitantly he reached up and felt in the darkness for the first handhold in the crumbling wall, while Otto gritted his teeth with the strain, feeling the raindrops beginning to beat against his bent back in ever-increasing fury.

Then the Count was gone and Otto breathed a sigh of relief. He straightened up and pressed himself tight against the wall, the raindrops erupting in little angry spurts around his feet. Men were scrambling up the wall everywhere. He could hear their grunts and groans and the stifled cries of pain as they ripped off a nail or knocked a shin against an overhang. He dismissed them. His heart beating furiously with the almost unbearable tension, he started to count off the seconds, eyes trying to penetrate the whirling wet gloom, alert for the first sign of danger.

Sixty! He flashed a look upwards. Against the fury of the rainstorm, he could just make out the Count's dark figure as he laboured to the top. It was time to go!

Five minutes later he and the Count, the others apparently lost in the fury of the howling storm, which reduced visibility to metres, had cleared the wall and were advancing across the rough broken ground outside, virtually feeling their way, hands extended like blind men, the wind whipping their clothes about them, the raindrops thrashing their faces furiously. But still, in spite of the sudden wet cold, Otto felt a warm glow begin to spread through his body. They had almost done it, he told himself excitedly. Almost!

Another minute passed. They could have been totally alone in the world. No other sound penetrated the storm save that of their own harsh laboured breathing, as they stumbled over rocks and slipped in the mud which was beginning to form everywhere. Suddenly the Count stiffened and stopped, holding up his arm warningly. Otto stopped immediately. 'What is it?' he hissed, his heart beating like a trip-hammer.

'There's . . . something to our front, Otto!' the Count hissed in a strangled voice.

Otto cocked his head against the roar of the wind, ignoring the bitter, cold raindrops slicing his skinny face. 'I can't hear—' he began and stopped short. Something was padding through the puddles to their immediate front and there was a strange metallic rattling noise!

He strained his eyes against the streaming white gloom, the raindrops threatening to blind him at any moment. Suddenly a dark low shape loomed up and Otto caught the dull silver gleam of a chain. Instinctively he knew what it was and his heart sank. It was a guard dog attached to a wire running around the perimeter of the Cage outside the wall. It was something he had not reckoned with one damned bit.

He gripped the Count's arm. Together they froze, the rain beating down upon them unheeded.

The dog came closer. Abruptly it stopped in its tracks. It raised its sloping head and sniffed the air. Suddenly it came – a long low growl that seemed to come from deep, deep down within its throat. Otto felt the small hairs at the back of his neck stand erect with fear. The beast had spotted them!

'The pistol?' the Count quavered.

'No,' Otto hissed back. 'Be a dead give-away. Let's see what it does.'

The dog was only a metre away now. In the rain-swept half-darkness Otto watched it stop, telling himself automatically that it was some kind of mongrel, a mixture of alsatian and wolf-hound, but it had the frightening long yellow teeth of both breeds; there seemed far too many of them for its vicious long snout, dripping now with saliva.

He swallowed hard, as the dog's ears stiffened and set back straight and close to its sloping head. He knew the signs. The beast was going to attack! Its upper lip rode up, baring the yellow teeth hideously. A low threatening growl started in its throat, a growl that Otto knew would turn into a harsh persistent yelping in one second flat. He swallowed the bitter hot bile that flooded his throat. He had to do it! Just as the beast opened his mouth to bark, he dived forward.

It grunted with surprise. Otto's hands clamped down hard on its snout from above and below, stifling the bark. The dog writhed furiously. Its right paw lashed out. Otto yelped with pain as the cruel claws ripped across his face, drawing blood immediately. The pain made him forget his fear. He was overcome with a burning rage at this damned animal which threatened to ruin the whole escape plan. He exerted all his strength, teeth gritted together furiously.

The animal writhed and tore to get free. Otto hung on. It weighed perhaps only half Otto's weight, but in its terror it dug in its hind legs and started to drag Otto through the mud and puddles. Desperately Otto tried to dig in his heels. But the ground was too slippery. He went down on his knees, head huddled in the animal's fur. His nostrils assailed by the stench of the animal. He felt like vomiting, but he must hang on. In a moment the animal would have dragged itself free and that would be that. With the last of his strength, hardly conscious of the Count's sudden yelp of alarm behind him, his face contorted with the effort, his shoulder muscles burning, he twisted.

Again the move caught the dog off guard. It stopped tugging him. Otto's sliding boots caught a grip. He increased his pressure. The dog yelped miserably through its clenched jaws. Otto had no mercy. The sweat and rain running down his strained face, he twisted and twisted. Madly the animal's paws scratched in the mud, sending up little spurts of water as it tried to break that killing grip. Otto held on for all he was worth, his breath coming in great hectic sobs. '*God, will you never die?*' he urged through gritted teeth. '*DIE!*'

The dog's struggles grew weaker and weaker. The right hind leg dropped. A moment later the other ceased its furious scratching. For a moment later, Otto held on, not trusting the hound. Finally he relaxed his grip on its muzzle, lifting his bloody lacerated hand slightly. Nothing happened. He relaxed the other. Still nothing. He let go. The hound dropped into the mud, its sightless eyes bulging. Gasping crazily, as if he had just won a great race, Otto slumped down in the mud, the blood from his ripped-open cheek falling in great scarlet gobs down his chest.

It was then a harsh American voice snarled, 'All right, Stahl, on ya feet! We ain't got all day, brother!'

Wearily, slowly, as if his head were worked by rusty springs, Otto looked up and gasped with shock.

The Count stood there, hands raised above his head. Next to him stood the little Italian-American, the rain streaming down his skinny dark face, Otto's pistol clenched in his fist . . .

FOUR

'I knew right from the start, ever since you were called away from the exercise yard that day, that you two guys were up to no good,' the Soldier explained triumphantly, as he expertly steered the little boat out of the cove and into the green heaving sea, the sky to the east already beginning to flush with the first dirty-grey light of the new day. He flung a quick glance to left and right and then snapped. 'All right, Kraut,' he jerked his pistol at Otto. 'Get up here and hold the rudder straight. Keep heading for that dark patch.' He indicated the dark smudge to their front which was mainland Italy. 'And no funny business, or your pal gets it first – then you – *in the nuts!*'

He stood up carefully, keeping Otto covered all the time, until he balanced his way to the rudder before moving forward and sitting down next to an ashen-faced Count, gun still held carefully in his skinny little hand.

'Ya see, the two of you were too damned secretive, always whispering together in corners like a couple of kids beating their meat or something. I knew you'd got a plan to get of that pen back there. It suited me to take orders from you for a while.'

He grinned wolfishly. 'Now *I* give the orders!'

Otto said nothing, as he tried to keep the boat straight which demanded quite a deal of strength, although the storm had passed and the water was no longer so choppy. The escape had been completely successful; it had gone according to plan. The home-made flare tossed at the Cage under the threat of the Soldier's gun had done the trick. Whistles had shrilled, flares had gone sailing into the sky in sudden alarm, machine-guns had chattered wildly, and everywhere in the suddenly glowing countryside the escapers had been running for cover in panic, while they had proceeded straight to the waiting boat. The only defect had been they were now under the Italian-American's command. Otto tensed against a particularly high wave, ducking as it splattered his face with icy spray, and asked, 'But what do you want with us? What use can we be to you? Back there are your people. They would have been more use to you than us.'

The Soldier laughed. It wasn't a pleasant sound. 'But there you're wrong, buster, dead wrong.' He jerked the pistol at Otto. 'You and this moth-eaten aristocrat here,' he indicated the Count who was now a deep sea-green colour and on the verge of being violently sick, 'are gonna be very useful to me.'

'Why?' Otto asked, intrigued in spite of the obvious danger; the man was a killer who would stop at nothing, that was for sure. When he needed the two friends no longer, he wouldn't hesitate to put a bullet through them – in the back.

The Italian-American countered with a question of his own. 'You Krauts heard of a guy named Skorzeny, *Otto Skorzeny*?'

The Count mumbled something, which the Soldier took to be a negative, and Otto shook his head. 'Should we have heard of him?' he asked.

The Soldier shrugged easily. 'It depends. Guys like me who are smart think he'd be a good joe to know, especially as he's carrying some one hundred thousand smackers – greenbacks to you jerks – to give away to the guy who can bring him a certain piece of information.'

'Piece of information?' Otto echoed stupidly.

'Sure.' The Soldier, smugly confident now that he was in complete charge and his little plan had worked, was much more talkative than normal.

'One hundred thousand dollars – for a name.'

'The name of what and who?'

'The name of the place where the Eyeties are hiding that creep Mussolini.'

'*Mussolini!*' Otto cried in surprise while next to the Soldier the Count leaned over the side of the bucking, heaving launch and began to vomit.

'You see,' the Italian-American explained as the little launch started to chug along the coast of the mainland with the red ball of the new sun burning away the rain so that the whole horizon seemed to be wreathed in a pink fog, 'my friends in Sicily have a lot of friends in Rome and everywhere in Italy. Nothing happens in Italy that we don't know about.'

Otto didn't say anything, but he could guess who those friends were – the Mafia.

'So as soon as Mussolini was kidnapped from the Grand Council Chamber, they started to follow his progress from hiding place to hiding place.[1] They figured that one day the information might come in useful to them.'

'Yes, I can just imagine how,' Otto said ironically, but irony was wasted on their captor.

'First they traced the route the kidnappers had taken until it seemed they had discovered where they were going to finally keep him, a little island called St Maddalena. But it didn't work out like that and the Krauts thought they'd bought a pup when they'd paid for info and found out *il Duce* wasn't there any more.' He clicked his forefinger back and forth a couple of times, as if he were working the trigger of a pistol. 'They didn't like it one bit and a couple of our soldiers went for a little walk and didn't come back.'

'Not the greatest loss to the world,' Otto said and the Count shot him a warning look.

[1] In the summer of 1943 the Grand Fascist Council turned from Mussolini, their leader, and looked to the Allies. Mussolini was instantly and mysteriously kidnapped as he left the council chamber.

'Button up your lip, Kraut,' the Soldier said threateningly, 'or you might go for the same little walk – *and not come back!* Well, to cut a long story short, my friends have found out the kidnappers' hiding place and this time it's for real. I was given the job of contacting this Skorzeny guy, who's acting personally for Hitler, and passing him the info. But there was a hitch.'

'Yes,' Otto said. 'You got put inside.'

'Yeah,' the Soldier agreed bitterly. 'After all we did for them damn ingrates, they crack down on our friends in Sicily, including Lucky Luciano, Three-Finger Harry and me and fling us in the slammer, just when we were in a position to make some real folding money for a change. That's what comes when you try to be patriotic and help yer country.' He spat into the sea.

'My heart bleeds for you,' Otto said. 'It could have happened to—'

Otto yelped suddenly with pain, as the Soldier lashed out and brought his free hand across Otto's injured cheek in a stinging blow which sent his head reeling to one side. 'I told ya to knock it off, didn't I?' he snarled. 'Next time, you jerk, I'll knock a couple of ya teeth out. *Now shut up!*'

Otto shut up, his eyes glowering with pain and suppressed rage, as he squatted there, with the Count's arm around his shoulder sympathetically, telling himself the little spaghetti-eater would pay for that blow.

'But why do you need us *now* that you've escaped? You're out of Sicily, you've got the boat, there's the mainland, and I'm sure we must be behind German lines now, so what purpose do we still serve?' the Count asked quickly, trying to draw their captor's attention away from Otto.

'Because you two guys are krauts. You know the lingo and the set-up, and I need somebody who can bargain with this *Oberstürmbannführer* Skorzeny guy for me.'

'*Oberstürmbannführer*?' the Count quavered, his face

suddenly very pale again. 'Is this . . . er . . . Skorzeny fellow a member of the SS?'

'Sure,' the Soldier answered easily. 'They are the kinda guys we could use in our organization, my friends and me,' he added in the strange way he had of always calling the Mafia his 'friends', as if even the mere mentioning of the organization would give away too much information.

'And where are we going to meet this *Oberstürmbannführer* Skorzeny?' the Count continued, recovering a little.

'Roma . . . Rome,' the Soldier snapped, his eyes fixed on the coast now, as he guided the rudder to port, 'now quit jawing and keep yer eyes on the shallows. We're going into land . . .'

It was unbearably hot in the capital for September and those Romans who could had fled the German-occupied city. Those who couldn't hid in the shade of their tree-lined courtyards and had taken refuge behind shuttered windows and barred doors. Even the blind lottery sellers with their monotonous chanting and the crippled ex-soldier beggars who normally bared their stumps for alms had vanished. Now the main streets of the capital had been abandoned to the skinny dogs who lay panting hectically in the dirty, overflowing gutters – and the hard-eyed sweating soldiers of General Student's Parachute Corps which had occupied the capital as soon as Italy had broken with its one-time ally and sued for peace with the Western Allies. Everywhere at strategic spots they had dug their guns in and occasionally the heavy brooding stillness that hung over the baking-hot streets was disturbed by the metallic rattle of their tanks, their decks laden with heavily armed, suspicious, trigger-happy paras.

'*Piniccella* time,' the Soldier commented on the heavy silence, 'that's what the Romans call their siesta time.' He nodded at their driver, a morose, cross-eyed individual who had seemingly appeared out of nowhere the day they had landed, after the Soldier had made a long-distance telephone call. But if the driver didn't say much, his looks were eloquent enough. They had better watch their step or there'd be trouble, serious trouble; and there was that big bulge under the cross-eyed driver's right arm which indicated he carried a gun in a holster. He was obviously one of the Soldier's 'friends'. Obediently Cross-Eyes turned into Via Pisanelli and began to head for the Tiber Embankment.

'So far those soldier boys of yours haven't given us much trouble,' the Soldier said, as the big black car rumbled down the empty silent street, 'but they're gonna check us out once we try to cross the Tiber. The word is they've got all nineteen bridges guarded so that they can keep check on anybody going up to the Piazza della Pilotta, below the Quirinale[1] where all their bigshots hang out.'

The Count flashed Otto a worried look. Otto knew why. If they fell into the hands of the German authorities they were in for trouble. Officially they were both posted as 'missing' after their flight from Russia.[2] But it wouldn't take the bulls long to trace their whole career and double-dealing since 1940, and the result of that would be inevitable: the chopping block and the official executioner in his dress suit and top hat, with his polite, 'I wonder if you wouldn't mind kneeling down over there, sir?' and the frightening last hiss of his axe.

The Soldier must have seen their looks, for he reached in the inside pocket of the natty new jacket which the cross-eyed chauffeur had brought with him and took out a piece of parchment, heavy with official seals and florid signatures. 'From the Commanding General of the *Carbinieri*,' he said triumphantly, 'certifying that we are good fascists, authorized by a known friend of the Reich to proceed through Rome without hindrance. You see, we

[1] The King of Italy's Palace
[2] See *Otto and the Reds* for further details

have friends everywhere.' He said something to Cross-Eyes and the chauffeur laughed coarsely.

Otto only half-heard, as the car swung into the Tiber Embankment running along the sluggish yellow river, considering their situation. The stubble-hoppers of the Army might well be easy to fool, but the SS would be different. They could and *would* ask awkward questions, such as what were two Germans doing in Rome although they belonged to no official organization, and why was Otto, a fit young man, not in the Army. He and the Count had to have something to offer them with no strings attached, such as the Soldier's demand for the 100,000 dollars for his information, which would make them out to be patriotic Germans of whom one did not ask awkward questions. He flashed the Count a look which said, 'Keep your trap shut for the moment', and said, 'How you gonna do this deal of yours? If you're gonna use us to put it across, how do you know that we won't just pass on the info to this SS *Oberstürmbannführer* and then let him know what kind of guy you are and have you arrested on the spot? It's one way of getting ourselves in sweet with the SS.'

The Soldier gave an ugly snigger and again said something to the chauffeur who laughed too, his contempt clearly obvious. 'Why, you crummy Kraut jerk, don't you think I ain't already thought of that? Jeez, what kind of dum-dum do you take me for?' he sneered. '*You're* gonna see *Oberstürmbannführer* Skorzeny on your lonesome. Me and Carlo here are gonna stay behind – with your moth-eaten aristocratic friend here,' he dug the Count in the ribs savagely. 'You're gonna tell Skorzeny what I've got to offer and where he can meet me with the dough. Try to double-cross me, brother, and your friend won't live long.'

Otto bit his bottom lip although he had somehow expected the Italian-American would pull a trick like this. 'But what if this Skorzeny doesn't want to play ball on your terms? What if when I put your proposition to him, he decides to run things his own way, take the information from you and then give you a nasty kick up your skinny wop arse – which you well deserve – and not give you the loot? What's to stop him?' Otto indicated the group of grim-faced paras in their camouflaged smocks and rimless helmets setting up a sandbagged machine-gun post on the embankment. 'The Germans have got everything pretty well sown up here, and I don't think even your *friends* are prepared to take on the *Wehrmacht* at this particular moment.'

Otto's veiled threats did not worry the Soldier. 'Don't make me piss down my leg,' he said coldly, his dark eyes flashing, '*Oberstürmbannführer* Skorzeny ain't gonna double-cross me, brother. Me and my friends know all about him. That guy's out for glory. He don't care about the smackers. All he wants is a name and no questions asked, believe you me. That big Kraut ain't gonna use *me*,' he jerked his thumb at his skinny chest, 'no problems . . .'

Otto's heart sank.

Oberstürmbannführer Skorzeny sweated. The whole back of his white too-tight sailor suit was black with sweat. But it wasn't the oppressive heat in the conference room which made him sweat so much; it was the fact that the whole Mussolini rescue operation and the glory that would go with it – and *Oberstürmbannführer* Otto Skorzeny dearly loved glory – was slipping out of his big hands.

Two weeks before Hitler had received the giant SS commando officer with his dark face, scarred from duelling as if a mad butcher had run amok with a hatchet, and pleaded with him to rescue his old friend Mussolini, tears in his eyes as he had done so. Now, not only had his search for the missing dictator been in vain, but the Army in the shape of General Student, 'the Conqueror of Holland', as he called himself proudly, and his paras were threatening to take over the whole operation.[1] The hard-faced shaven-headed General, whose forehead still bore the ugly red scar of the bullet wound he had received in Rotterdam in May 1940, was a glory-hunter just as he was, the big SS man knew that well enough, and he had far more resources at his disposal than did Skorzeny. If he didn't get a tip-off soon, Student would find the missing Duce himself and that would be the end of his personal hopes to cure his throat-ache at last. Nervously he fingered his neck as if he could already feel the Knight's Cross, which would cure his throat-ache, hanging there as he listened to Student lecturing the officers packed into the hot room.

'Gentlemen, we can now rule out the possibility that the spaghetti-eaters are keeping the Duce somewhere off the mainland in one of those islands of theirs. It would be too dangerous with the Allies now in virtual control of the seaways to and from Italy.' He nodded at the big SS member clad in the too-tight sailor's uniform. '*Oberstürmbannführer* Skorzeny there can take off his nice sailor suit now. There'll be no more little boats to play with, I'm afraid.'

The hard-bitten para officers laughed raucously and Skorzeny's scarred sallow face flushed a deep red. For weeks now he had been acting the role of a drunken sailor in various coastal ports in an attempt to find which island the Italians had taken the missing dictator to. For weeks now he had been plagued with a rotten headache from the cheap wine he had been forced to drink in those rough waterfront bars and a bad case of the 'thinshits', as he called it, from the contaminated muck they served in such places. 'What makes you think he's on the mainland, General?' he forced himself to say.

Student gave a false smile. 'Two things,' he barked in that nasal Prussian manner of his which made Skorzeny's skin crawl. As a Viennese, he hated everything Prussian.

[1] In 1940 Student's para-troopers had played the main role in the conquest of Holland

'One, the fact the Allies control the seaways. Two, it has been reported by agents that General Soleti of the *Carbinieri*, who we are sure knows where Mussolini is being kept, is sending supplies out of Rome *secretly* into the Italian Appenines to the north of here. It would be an ideal place to keep a prisoner. Who goes into the mountains in summer when there is no skiing? Further, roads are few and far between. It wouldn't be too difficult to guard someone up there with only a handful of men. A man and boy, *even if they were Macaronis*, could hold some of those passes against an army!' Dutifully the para officers laughed at their CO's comment on the Italians and one of them asked, 'But the Apennines cover a large area, *Herr General*, and we haven't got all the time in the world. Any day now the spaghetti-eaters could hand over the Duce to the Western Allies.'

Student winked knowingly. 'I have already thought of that, Maas. As you know I am an old *Luftwaffe* man myself and, as they say, one hand washes the other. For a case of champus, I've convinced the CO of the 82nd Reconnaissance Wing stationed at Lake Bracciano to set his fly-boys off on an aerial survey. And what do you think they are going to survey? Eh?'

'The Apennines, *Herr General!*' his officers roared back as one and Skorzeny told himself the sow-Prussians were always so noisy; they invariably spoke as if they were shouting orders across some kilometre-broad barracks square. The noise was bad for his nerves; he didn't like it one bit.

'Yes,' Student went on confidently, tapping the big map of Italy with his knuckles, 'I have every confidence that it can be only a matter of days, perhaps even hours now, before the fly-boys discover where the Macaronis are hiding the Duce. Then, gentlemen, we shall go in and snatch him up from beneath their very noses. How?' He laughed, 'Why, the way paras always go in. From the sky. And I don't need to remind you fellows that there'll be tin in this, plenty of it!'

Spontaneously the assembled officers broke into the para-troop song, *The Sun Shone Red*, stamping their heavy boots enthusiastically in time to the song.

It was too much for Otto Skorzeny. The noise deafened him and ominous threatening rumbles had commenced in his plagued stomach. He fled and General Student called after him, 'Goodbye, sailor. Don't forget to kiss the captain for me!'

It was thus that Otto Stahl had his first meeting with the man who was going to play a significant role in his life for the next two years in the not very salubrious setting of the temporary officers' thunderboxes erected behind Student's HQ. 'Skorzeny?' he asked the groaning man bent double over the thunderbox, a small mountain of newspaper squares held at the ready in his right hand, sweat pouring down his scarred face. '*Obersturmbannführer* Otto Skorzeny?'

The officer, who for some reason was wearing a sailor suit which was much too small for him, groaned miserably and said weakly, 'Go away, go away please. Can't a fellow even have a moment's privacy. Oh, my God,' he moaned as he was racked by another spasm. 'How beastly you Prussians are! You have absolutely no sense of shame!'

Otto frowned at the reference to the Prussians. As a Berliner he supposed he was nominally a Prussian. He took another look at the groaning giant in his sailor suit. Was he like *that*, he wondered, even though he was nearly two metres tall and his face looked as if a drunkard had tried to make mince-meat of it with a blunt carving knife. Still the urgency of his mission was too great. 'My name's Stahl,' he persisted, 'Otto Stahl. I used – *no, I work*,' he corrected himself hastily, 'for the *Abwehr* here in Rome.'

'So,' Skorzeny groaned without interest, shaking as the

spasm ran its course. 'God in heaven, I deserve to be drawn and quartered if I ever eat another lasagne!'

'I have information,' Otto went on desperately, thinking of the Count being held at the far end of the *Ponte Milvio*, the bridge across the Tiber, at the mercy of the Soldier and Cross-Eyes, 'vital information.'

'Information?' Skorzeny croaked, looking up and taking in the handsome blond young man with the open winning face and the keen blue eyes staring down at him, 'What kind of information?'

Otto hesitated for only a moment. 'About Benito Mussolini,' he answered.

'You mean—' Skorzeny let the heap of paper fall, his 'thinshits' forgotten.

'Yes, where they are keeping him.'

'Tell me.' Skorzeny almost rose in his excitement, but remembered just in time that that was impossible. 'In three devils' name, Herr Stahl, tell me where they are keeping him! I'll give you anything you want – *money*.'

Otto's eyes flickered greedily for a moment, but he knew to demand money now would be wrong. 'No, *Obersturmbannführer*,' he declared proudly while a little voice at the back of his brain said mockingly, 'Oh what a fine red arsehole you are, Otto, lad, I do this not for filthy lucre but for Germany and our beloved Führer.' He shot up his right arm and cried, '*Heil Hitler!*'

Sitting on his wooden thunderbox, not even minding the row for once, *Obersturmbannführer* Skorzeny shot up his massive arm and echoed the greeting, sitting at attention as regulations demanded. Contact had been made successfully . . .

FIVE

The little squad of SS commandos caught the Soldier and Cross-Eyes completely by surprise. Cross-Eyes was urinating luxuriously into the sluggish yellow waters of the Tiber and the Soldier was cleaning his nails casually with the point of the stiletto he usually carried in the side of his boot, when the Volkswagen jeep swung round the corner and skidded to a stop a dozen metres away.

The Soldier saw Otto's grinning face and took in the situation at once. 'Carlo!' he cried urgently and threw the thin-bladed knife.

The driver sitting next to Otto yelped with pain and slammed back against the wall of the cab, ashen-faced, a knife protruding from his right shoulder. Otto flung himself to the ground in the same instant that Cross-Eyes standing next to the River Tiber fired. A slug cut the air just above his head. Skorzeny tugged furiously at his pistol, but Otto beat him to it. Crouched low at the side of the car, he fired and the Italian staggered backwards, arm flailing. With a splash he went into the Tiber. For one fleeting second he reached the surface again and then he was gone.

'Watch the old man with the white hair!' Otto yelled furiously as the other SS commandos tumbled out of the back of the VW jeep and went into action, firing from the hip as they pelted forward.

Next to the Soldier the Count ducked as lead cut the air all around him.

'That's it!' Otto cried enthusiastically. 'Keep yer turnip down—'

The rest of his words were drowned by the high-pitched

rapid burr of a machine-pistol. The Soldier trying to flee the car screamed shrilly. His back disappeared in a red welter of blood and shattered bone. He staggered on a few paces, hands outstretched falteringly in front of him like an old blind man trying to find his way; then abruptly without warning his whole body trembled uncontrollably. Next instant he hit the cobbles with a thud. Otto ran towards him and, his face contorted with disgust, turned the soldier over with the toe of his boot. The Soldier's sightless eyes stared up at him. A trickle of black blood curled out of the pinched white nostrils.

'Dead?' Skorzeny inquired a little anxiously, pistol in hand for now he had finally succeeded in drawing it.

'Dead,' Otto echoed.

'Oh I say,' Skorzeny said in a thick voice and reached hastily for the handkerchief which he always kept tucked up his sleeve. 'How unfortunate!' Holding it tightly clasped to his nose, he stepped over the dead Soldier and advanced on the Count, who had now popped up his head once again, grinning with relief. 'Skorzeny, Otto,' he said formally, '*Obersturmbannführer SS*,' adding in the Viennese fashion, 'Kiss the hand, Count.'

'Kiss the hand, *Obersturmbannführer*,' the Count replied happily, rising to the bait immediately.

Inwardly Otto groaned. He could see what was going to happen. The old fart had found a new model. Soon he would be all old-school Viennese aristocrat with lace handkerchieves, gallant manners, 'kiss yer thigh, Countess,' and all the rest of that Old Austrian soft-soap.

Neither Skorzeny or the Count noticed; they were both taken up with each other, busy passing Viennese compliments back and forth until Otto grunted, 'Oh fer Chrissake, kiss and shut up! Tell him, Count, tell him where they're keeping the Duce bloke.'

The Count beamed at Otto, then at his new friend. 'Of course, of course, Otto, my dear chap, I'd completely forgotten.' He turned to the scar-faced SS giant. 'The Gran

Sasso d'Italia,' he announced triumphantly, 'that's where they're keeping him.'

'In the Apennines?'

'Yes.'

Skorzeny frowned. 'Then we've got to move quickly before it's too late.'

'*We?*' Otto asked sternly.

'Yes, of course,' Skorzeny answered, tucking away his lace handkerchief. 'From this moment on, you are both naturally honorary members of the SS. I mean,' he flashed Otto a winning smile, 'with your name Stahl,[1] you should have been in the SS long ago. *Nomen is omen*, after all.'

Otto groaned. They had landed in the shit yet again . . .

Skorzeny was the centre of things once again and Otto standing at the back of the operations room crowded with the tough-looking para officers in their baggy sand-coloured trousers could see that General Student did not like it one bit. Nor for that matter did he, now that he knew what Skorzeny's little plan was. Skorzeny indicated the big map of Northern Italy. 'Monte Carno of Gran Sasso,' he announced, 'three thousand metres above the plain below, the highest point in the Apennines. Here, at its foot is the plateau of Campo Imperatore some 2,000 metres high, which has always been a favourite with Italian skiers.'

Student snorted, obviously irritated with the SS officer, but he made no further objection as Skorzeny continued.

'Now my sources inform me,' Skorzeny winked at Otto, 'that the Duce is being held at the one resort hotel there is on the Campo Imperatore, to which the sole access is by funicular which runs 1,000 metres straight up from the village of Assergi, and around Assergi all roads have been blocked by *carbinieri* who are loyal to the government, which means they are loyal to the Western Allies. So the

[1] Otto's surname 'Stahl' means 'steel'

only way that we can get Mussolini out of the Hotel Campo Imperatore is by air.'

Student spoke at last. 'Of course, *Obersturm*, we understand that. After all we are para-troopers. *In*, we can go,' he paused momentarily, 'The question is how do we get *out*?'

Skorzeny lied easily. 'I have thought about that, too, *Herr General*,' he said. 'Naturally your brave fellows will be able to get in, though by glider incidentally and not by parachute – the thermals would swirl most of them into the terrible mountain fissures below Monte Carno—'

'Yes, yes,' Student butted impatiently. 'I understand all that, but how do we get the Duce out?'

Skorzeny beamed at the heavily-set para general. 'Isn't it obvious?'

'No, it isn't!'

Glibly Skorzeny lied again, exerting all his Viennese charm, 'By the funicular railway of course.'

'The funicular?'

'Naturally. The *carbinieri* will be expecting an attack from the base of the thing at the village of Assergi. But will they anticipate one from above, especially if we ensure they get no warning by cutting all the telephones wires linking the two stations?'

Student was impressed. 'I must say, Skorzeny, that it is a devilishly cunning idea! They won't expect us coming down from 3,000 metres right on top of them, of course they won't! Excellent. I shall lead the attack personally.'

Only Otto saw the sudden worried look which appeared fleetingly in Skorzeny's dark eyes; but then he and the SS officer had discussed that very possibility only hours before when they had worked out their little plan. Indeed he, Otto, had been the one who had suggested a way out if Student decided to take part in the risky airborne mission. Now Skorzeny used Otto's suggestion. 'I would be a very happy man, General Student, if you would deign to carry out that task,' he commenced in that smooth Viennese way of his, oozing charm from every pore. 'Then I'd know that the operation could simply not fail. Your outstanding record, *Herr General*, in Holland, Crete and half a dozen other battlefields is proof enough of that.'

Student beamed red-faced with pride. 'Say no more, my dear Skorzeny,' he puffed, holding up his hand. 'Say no more.'

'However, my dear General,' Skorzeny continued, 'that, I am afraid, cannot be.'

Student's happy look vanished abruptly. 'What was that?' he rapped.

'You personally cannot go, *Herr General*. I simply could not let you risk your great reputation if anything goes wrong.'

'Risk my great reputation?' Student asked, suddenly cautious.

'Yes, General. Before I left Berlin, the Führer said this to me.' There was a hushed intake of breath at the mention of the Führer and Skorzeny paused for an instant before he continued, 'He said – and I quote, gentlemen – "My friend Mussolini has to be rescued at once. But understand that if you fail, I may have to disown you since Italy is our ally – in name, at least. I should have to say – for reasons of state – that you acted without orders. Your foolhardy action was prompted by excessive zeal, by ambition. If you fail, I must repudiate you, Skorzeny. You must accept this heavy responsibility for the sake of Germany." '

The words had their effect. Student suddenly licked his dry lips and Otto could read his mind, for he now only too clearly understood the way the military mind worked. Suddenly the worried General was visualizing the perks and honours that went with being a general vanish, the relegation to some third-class spa to spend the rest of his life in civilian obscurity, the days of glory gone for ever; no more personal thunderboxes with officer sentries to guard them; no more heel-clicking and saluting; brass bands and 'turn out the guard'; no more champagne parties in the mess and high-class mistresses in black silk underwear –

just mother in her homespun and beer and an occasional schnapps if you were lucky.

'Of course, of course, Skorzeny, you are quite right,' Student said at last. 'A general should never command from the front. I shall leave it up to you, my dear fellow. But as soon as the Duce is rescued you must bring him *personally* to my HQ here, I charge you with that.'

Skorzeny clicked his heels together and bent slightly at the waist, as if he were a Viennese waiter taking an order for one of those sickly cakes they constantly ate in the Austrian capital and said, 'Your wish is my command, *Herr General*.'

'Good then, I'm glad that is understood. Now then, gentlemen, let us look at what we've got. The Parachute Division has about twelve DFS 230 gliders here in Italy and a squadron of Heinkel IIIs to tow them.' He made a quick calculation. 'That means with your SS commandos, Skorzeny, we could put in a team of one hundred and eight combat soldiers altogether. Not many, I admit, but surprise will be on our side. By the time the spaghetti-eaters wake up to what is happening, it will be all over . . .'

Otto let Student's briefing recede into the distance, while he mulled over that part of the plan unknown to the General, who, if it worked out as they had planned, was in for the biggest surprise of his long and distinguished career. How had the Count put it at the end of their own little briefing session when the plan had been finalized? 'Then, my dear *Obersturm*, like the young fellow in the Greek legend, we will grow wings and fly away.' Skorzeny and the Count, the silly old fart, had laughed uproariously. Otto hadn't, for it had just struck him that Icarus had flown too close to the sun. He had suffered a very nasty accident indeed as a result. 'Let's hope the sodding wax don't melt this time,' he whispered fervently to himself.

'Did you say something, Otto?' the Count standing next to him asked sotto voce.

'No, no, I was just saying my prayers, that's all . . .'

SIX

In Room 201, his low-ceiling one-room apartment in the Hotel Campo Imperatore, Benito Mussolini, hollow-eyed and unshaven, his black eyes seemingly enormous in his sallow face, waited impatiently until the scruffy old shepherd finished the cards.

His guards allowed the old man in every day now to keep their prisoner company and read the cards for him; for the Duce was desperate to know what was going to happen to him. He clutched at any straw, even that offered by the ignorant peasant sheepherder, who was tending his flocks at his nearby summer pasturage.

'Well?' he snapped, unable to contain his impatience any longer, as old Nisi laid out the cards on the table with gnarled stiff fingers, bent with years of hard work, 'what do they say?'

Nisi looked up a little cunningly at the former dictator, dressed in a creased shiny blue suit, his shoes scuffed and broken. 'You are due,' he said slowly, flashing his eyes from the cards to the prisoner and back again, 'to be rescued . . . in . . . rather romantic circumstances . . . that is what the cards say . . .'

Mussolini sprang to his feet, thrusting out his impressive black jaw in the pose of his great days. 'Rubbish,' he cried, 'absolute rubbish, you peasant fool!' With a sudden blow, he swept the cards to the floor. 'You and your damned false prophecies. You are just trying to make a fool of me.' He began to pace up and down nervously.

The shepherd looked at him a little sorrowfully and slowly began to pick up his cards. 'I just tell you what they say, sir,' he said pocketing them. 'I'll come again tomorrow.'

There was a knock on the door. It was opened by Lieutenant Faiola, the commander of the seventy-strong security guard.

Mussolini's eyes lit up when he saw the smart-looking young officer, for he knew he had just returned from the capital where he had gone for fresh instructions. 'What are my Romans doing, Faiola?' he demanded in his old imperial style.

'Looting, Duce,' the young officer answered brutally, as the shepherd touched his forelock and passed out of the room.

'I don't mean the looters,' Mussolini said with a gesture of irritation, 'I mean my true fascists.'

Faiola flashed him a brilliant, white-toothed smile, 'Frankly, Duce, I didn't meet any. I think they've all reformed. Now, sir, about your lunch . . .'

Just before he turned the corner of the corridor, Nisi flung a look at the couple standing at the door and told himself Mussolini looked old and very sad; but then, he thought, he'd had a good run for his money with all those society dames falling into his bed with their legs wide open before the Duce could even get his pants down. And with this thought he dismissed the Duce and went out into the open.

The sun shone brilliantly and the cold stark spur of the Monte Corno glistened. He narrowed his eyes. Two dark shadows seemed to be hovering in the sky close to the peak. Eagles? he queried. They could be dangerous for his lambs. It wasn't unknown for a mountain eagle to come swooping down and pick off a stray lamb. He'd have to keep an eye on them. Then he started to plod back to his flock in the steady slow gait of the countryman who knows that he's got all the time in the world, for Mother Nature was never rushed. Behind him yet another dark shape appeared in the hard blue wash around the Monte Corno . . .

'In the old days in Vienna,' the Count was saying, 'life was good if you were rich and belonged to society. I remember old Baron vom Gerlach, for instance, one day throwing a waiter out of the window of a café because he'd served the wrong kind of coffee – the Viennese have at least thirty kinds, you know, Otto.' He sighed. 'Happy days, Otto, happy days.'

'Oh shut up, you silly old shit,' Otto snapped thickly, feeling his stomach roll unpleasantly, as the big glider gave a sudden lurch as it hit another thermal above the mountains. 'I can't hear myself think with you rabbiting on like that.'

The Count was in no way offended. 'Not feeling so well, Otto, what?' he said cheerfully, looking around the glider packed with paras dressed in green overalls, their tough bodies laden with lethal weapons of all sorts. 'Can't say it affects me—'

'The tow plane's casting off – *now!*' the glider pilot's urgent warning cut into the Count's words. 'Hold tight everywhere!' Hastily the paras and the handful of SS men grabbed the nearest spar, as somewhere ahead the towing plane released the twenty metre towing rope and the glider lurched sickeningly.

Otto closed his eyes and fought desperately against the bitter green bile which welled up in his throat and threatened to choke him.

Now the only sound was the hiss of the wind in the ears and that of Skorzeny's knife as he started to slit the glider's canvas in order to get a better view of the terrain below.

Otto steeled himself and forced his eyes open. Through the hole Skorzeny was cutting he could just see a squat white horseshoe-shaped building taking shape, with beyond a sheer drop. 'My God,' he said thickly, 'if we miss the—' he didn't finish his sentence, not daring to think through that particular horrifying thought. Instead he closed his eyes tightly, his ears full of the hiss of the wind.

'*Helmets on!*' Skorzeny barked. '*Feet up!*'

Mechanically Otto did as commanded, his eyes still tightly screwed together, while all around him the paras raised their feet from the floor.

'*Thirty seconds to landing!*' the sweating pilot cried a little hysterically, as he fought the controls, trying to avoid the boulders which littered the plateau everywhere.

'*Crash landing!*' Skorzeny yelled, his terrified gaze taking in the landing strip below, from which sheep were scattering in panic. It looked more like a damned abandoned ski slope. It would be madness to attempt to land on that.

The glider's nose came up. The paras slammed against their seats.

'Here we go!' the Count called joyfully, as the glider's skids hit the ground with a thump and the wooden and canvas plane hurtled across the plateau in a great cloud of dust, swaying and shuddering, pieces falling of it like splintered matchwood, the barbed wire wrapped around the skids to shorten the sliding distance snapping like twine. Then with a great howl of brakes and the rending and tearing of canvas, it gave one huge last lurch and came to a halt, the sunlight suddenly flooding into the fuselage through the massive holes which had appeared everywhere and blinding them.

'*RAUS!*' Skorzeny yelled.

The paras needed no urging. They tumbled out of the wrecked glider and started to double for the hotel, as yet another huge shape came winging its way in to chance destruction on the boulder-littered plateau. Otto felt someone seize him and push him outside, his eyes still tightly clasped together, his stomach rolling furiously like thunder heralding a violent storm. He dropped on the grass. The boots of the racing paras receded into the distance, but

Otto could not move. He simply lay there paralysed with fear.

After what seemed an age, he felt something wet and warm on his face. For one horrifying moment he thought it was blood. He opened his eyes. A black collie was licking his face in a friendly manner, while behind it there hovered an anxious leather-faced Italian in the ankle-length fur coat of a shepherd. '*Giornio*,' he said obviously relieved that Otto was not dead, but otherwise apparently not surprised at these winged monsters which had so suddenly appeared out of nowhere on this still September afternoon. '*Bello, si?*' he swept his gnarled paw around the scene. '*Molto bello, no?*' He beamed down at Otto, as if he were the official representative of the local tourist board.

Otto closed his eyes. There was nothing else he could think of doing. Happily the collie started to lick his face once again. Thus it was that while the greatest rescue operation of World War Two was taking place, Otto Stahl lay on his back on a mountain meadow, while a black dog licked his face and an old peasant expounded on the beauties of the Apennian scenery . . .

Pandemonium reigned. Whistles shrilled. Half dressed *carbinieri* ran back and forth down the Hotel's corridors. Guard dogs barked frantically. Officers startled from their midday siesta yelled orders and counter-orders.

The paras with Skorzeny in the lead surged forward cheering. A well-known face appeared fleetingly at an upper window. '*Heil Duce!*' they yelled excitedly before Mussolini was dragged out of sight.

The SS officer clattered up the steps into the main lobby. A group of *carbinieri* in green-grey uniforms sweated fearfully as they attempted to set up the tripod for a heavy machine-gun. Skorzeny, followed by a panting Count, clubbed his way through them, scattering the much smaller Italians like skittles to both sides as he ran on.

'*Mani in alto!*' the Count croaked, enjoying this new 'adventure' in spite of the physical exertion, and pleased to see the *carbinieri* shooting up their hands in surrender.

Skorzeny pounded up a marble staircase, taking the steps three at a time, the Count floundering after him. His would be the honour of liberating Il Duce. Nothing could stop him now.

An Italian colonel with a beard peered round a corner. Before Skorzeny could react, the Count shouted '*Mani in alto!*' again, thrusting up his pistol, which was still on safety, threateningly.

'Surrender!'

The Italian Colonel ducked back into his room. An instant later he reappeared bearing a goblet of red wine in his trembling hands. 'To the victor,' he said in hesitant German, and with a bow proferred it.

Skorzeny and the Count took token sips, hoping that the wine had not been poisoned. Then ran on.

Some instinct told the Count to open the door of Room 201. In the centre of the room, three men stared at the white-haired man in the ill-fitting parachute uniform, with the camouflage net of his helmet trailing down over his forehead like a green veil, dumbfounded.

The Count did not recognize the two younger men, but he recognized the one standing between them. He had seen him once before in 1930 standing in his customary heroic pose on the balcony of the Palazzo Venezia. The Count clicked to attention and his hand shot out in the Roman salute. '*Evviva il Duce!*' he snapped and then turned to the big man standing behind him. 'Il Duce, may I present to you *Obersturmbannführer* Skorzeny from Berlin?' he said with appropriate formality.

Skorzeny was well aware of the historic importance of this moment. He knew instinctively it would be the most significant sixty seconds of his life; it would change everything. Elbowing the Count to one side, and with a fine instinct for an entrance line, he sprang to attention and cried, 'Duce, the Führer sent me! *You're free!*'

Mussolini, overcome with emotion, stumbled forward, the tears streaming down his pale face. Fervently he embraced the Viennese giant and then reaching up on tiptoe planted a wet kiss on both his flushed cheeks, crying, 'I knew my friend Adolf Hitler would not leave me in the lurch! I knew!' Then he turned and kissed the Count.

Outside the *carbinieri* were applauding happily as yet another glider came hurtling in, as if they were spectators at a theatrical performance put on for their special benefit.

Now that the action was over Otto pushed away the collie and rose to his feet, shaking his head, as the *Wehrmacht* movie cameramen rose from their cover and began photographing the applauding *carbinieri* and the happy sweating paras who were slumped on the cropped grass everywhere now. War, he concluded, seemed to be one big publicity exercise. Slowly he started to walk to the hotel, pushing his way through the bleating sheep. In five minutes the last phase of the operation would begin and he didn't want to be left behind on that remote plateau once the paras discovered they had been tricked.

It was now three in the afternoon. The main body of the paras were beginning to assemble ready for their attack on the funicular station some two kilometres from the hotel; the wires that linked the place with the plain below had already been cut and they were confident that they would achieve complete surprise.

Meanwhile Skorzeny's handful of SS men were busy on the plateau itself, draping a path between the wrecked gliders with the hotel's sheets, finishing up by forming a crude arrow to the south of the Monte Corno, watched by the handful of curious *carbinieri* who had not been locked inside the hotel's basement.

'How much space have we got, Otto?' Skorzeny asked

after the young Berliner had finished pacing out the sheeted path.

'Seventy-five metres to the best of my knowledge,' Otto replied.

Skorzeny's brow creased in a worried frown. 'Even for them that's precious little, Otto,' he commented. 'It's going to be damnably difficult,' he explained. 'We can't take off in the direction of the Monte Corno. Instead we'll have to do it with a north-west wind howling behind us, engines going full throttle, brakes on until the very last moment. With luck we'll be airborne before the runway peters out. Otherwise,' he didn't complete the rest of the sentence. He didn't need to, for Otto knew exactly what would happen; they would go over the edge of the ravine and smash to their deaths hundreds of metres below.

'It's either that or them, *Obersturm*,' Otto said, jerking his thumb at the heavily armed paras grouping around their officers ready for the surprise attack. 'If we don't pull it off, I, for one, don't fancy facing that hairy-arsed bunch of stubble-hoppers.'

Skorzeny nodded his agreement. 'Yes, Otto, you're right. That lot are a law unto themselves. If they think their beloved Pappa Student is being tricked, I am sure that they'd show no mercy.' He shuddered dramatically. 'Otto, you'd better go inside and bring out the Duce. They're due in at any moment now.'

Otto hurried away, just as the first soft noise of radial engines indicated that the two Storch recce planes were dead on time. Skorzeny's bribe of ten thousand American dollars each; a case of bubbly; and the two best whores available in Vienna's Tenth District had worked; the *Luftwaffe* pilots were keeping their promise.

Mussolini was already dressed for the trip. Now he was clad in a shabby blue topcoat and soft brown felt hat. He stood in front of the mirror in his room, pulling up the collar of the coat and then turning it down again, each time turning his profile in a different direction as he tried to calculate the impression he made. Occasionally he would thrust up his black jowl in the posture Otto remembered well from the pre-war newsreels, or lower his head into the collar so that his dark burning eyes were highlighted and created the fullest possible effect.

'Herr Duce,' Otto said hesitantly, feeling somehow foolish. 'We must be going. The planes are landing.' He indicated the two monoplanes coming in for a bumpy landing.

'Just one moment, young man,' Mussolini said severely in quite good German. He thrust his right hand inside his heavy coat and frowned hard. 'How does that look, eh? Napoleon returning from Elba. Do you think that would impress Herr Hitler? Or this?' The sombre frown disappeared at once and the hand came from within his coat. He beamed, showing more teeth than Otto thought possible for a human being to possess, head held high and at an affected angle. 'March on Rome look, 1922 . . . Would that be more optimistic and impress the Führer better?' He waited expectantly, holding the pose with difficulty for Otto's benefit.

'The March on Rome look, 1922,' Otto said hurriedly. 'The Führer always likes confident people around him.'

'Good, so be it. Here – my suitcase. Be careful to keep it upright – it contains my make-up bottles.'

Thus laden Otto followed the posturing dictator outside, while his one-time captors cried '*Evviva!*' and the two *Luftwaffe* pilots, their faces fully reflecting their horror at what lay before them, revved their engines furiously.

Skorzeny was arguing with the pilot of the first plane shouting above the racket of the motor, 'If anything happens to the Duce let it be my responsibility!'

Mussolini heard the remark and faltered, but Otto smiled reassuringly, and perhaps assuming that he had misunderstood the German he continued his progress to the leading plane.

'All right,' the pilot cried in exasperation, 'Well, for God's sake, let's get on with it!' Suddenly he became aware of Otto and the Duce, the former sweating with the effort of carrying the Italian's heavy suitcase. 'Oh, thou holy strawsack,' he groaned slapping his forehead, 'don't tell me he's taking *that* with him too?'

'It is my make-up,' Mussolini replied severely. 'I cannot be expected to meet your Führer without my make-up. It would be impossible to let him see me thus, so pale, so thin in the face, so sick.' Mussolini sucked in his cheeks and gave a sad-eyed wan look, as if he were in the last stages of galloping consumption.

Skorzeny reacted quickly. 'Of course, Duce, the young man will bring it in the second plane.' He nodded swiftly at Otto, who understood what he was to do with the Italian's precious make-up when the Duce wasn't looking. 'Now, with all due respect, we must be off!' He almost bundled the Italian into the plane, and then forced his own enormous two hundred pound bulk after him.

The pilot revved his engine again furiously. Across the way the paras preparing to attack the funicular station turned curiously. Otto flashed them a look. They were murmuring angrily (he thought) to themselves. A sergeant had unslung his machine-pistol. The noise coming from the Storch's radial was ear-splitting, with the whole plane quivering with the strain, as if it were some highly strung horse at the starter's gate impatient to be off.

The plane started to roll forward, bouncing frighteningly over the uneven, rock-littered ground. It juddered and shivered down the incline at a hundred and fifty kilometres an hour, getting ever closer to the drop at the far end, but still not airborne. The Count muttered in an awe-stricken voice, 'Oh, my God!' and crossed himself in the elaborate Austrian Catholic fashion. Otto clenched his hands into tight, painful fists. *Would the shitting Storch never take off?* The edge of the ravine came closer and closer.

Five metres from the drop, the pilot put his flaps down, trying to bring the Storch up, yanking with all his strength at the stick. The Count closed his eyes. Abruptly with an unholy jar, the plane's right wheel struck a rock. Otto gasped. The left wing canted downwards crazily. Otto knew it was all over. Nothing could save Mussolini and Skorzeny now. They'd be over the edge in a flash. Next instant the Storch bounced crookedly off the edge of the tremendous drop. It plummeted towards the valley one thousand metres below like a lift out of control. Even the paras were awed into silence. Otto tensed, ears straining for the crash of the plane smashing into the valley floor.

But it wasn't to be. Mussolini was fated to live another few years before the mob would lynch him and the Italian women who had once clamoured for his favours in bed would spread their legs and urinate on his dead, contorted face. Suddenly the little plane soared into sight again, stark black against the bright yellow of the afternoon sun. 'They've done it!' the Count cried excitedly, '*they've done it!*'

In that same instant the paras, realizing how they had been tricked, erupted in fury. A wild burst of machine-pistol fire came cutting the air in the direction of the two friends and Otto awoke suddenly to their own danger. He dropped Mussolini's case. It burst open scattering bottles and tubes of make-up everywhere. 'Come on!' he cried as the paras surged forward in battle formation, grabbing the Count's hand, 'or those stubble-hoppers'll have the eggs off us!'

Frantically they piled into the plane, the pilot gunning his engine furiously. Next moment they were on their way too, bumping across that uneven plateau to chance that death-defying plunge over the lip of the ravine, followed by the angry fire of the betrayed para-troopers . . .

ENVOI

Mussolini had gone now. The Führer had wanted to see him urgently. A new fascist republic had to be founded in Northern Italy to bolster up the German hold on that part of the country. Now Skorzeny and his two new recruits to the *Waffen SS* Captain Count von der Weide and Lieutenant Otto Stahl were left to their own devices in far-away Vienna, fêted by the press and radio, enjoying their time off.

On this warm, late September day, they lounged in Skorzeny's palatial hotel suite, drinking ice-cold Hungarian Tokay wine, the newspapers praising the bold rescue attempt tossed everywhere, listening to Dr Goebbels, the Minister of Propaganda, harangue his listeners in far off Berlin over the radio. 'In spite of the base treachery of the scum around Marshal Badoglio,[1] Providence and Major Skorzeny have ensured that the Duce, Rome's greatest son, will continue to fight on our side.'

The Count, who had had his white hair cropped and whose face was covered with sticky plaster where he had cut himself with his razor in the fond hope of obtaining scars such as those adorning Skorzeny's face, beamed at their new boss, 'Excellent, Chief, what!' he barked in his 'SS voice', as he called it.

Skorzeny lowered his eyes modestly, while Otto looked down bored at the newspaper photo of some peasant girl in a low-cut frock presenting flowers to a triumphant Skorzeny.

'As long as Germany can produce soldiers of the calibre of Otto Skorzeny and his brave men, I, for one, have no fears for the future,' the little club-footed dwarf shrilled

[1] Head of the group of Italians who had deposed Mussolini

into the microphone of the Berlin *Sportpalast* and the Count beamed even more at the mention of 'his brave men'; he pushed out his chest proudly.

'Come what may – be it half the world against us, *Greater Germany must and will win this war!*' Goebbels screamed his final words at the audience. '*SIEG HEIL!*'

Skorzeny, the sensitive Viennese, winced at the noise and as the brass band crashed into the *Horst Wessel Lied*, the marching song of the National Socialist Party, he slung his long booted legs from his chair and hurriedly turned the radio off. 'I must say you Prussians do make a devil of a racket, even in a good cause,' he said to Otto, fingering his newly won Knight's Cross, the pride of his life.

Otto grunted something unintelligible and the Count, as enthusiastic as ever, said, 'But it's all in a good cause, *Obersturm*. Every bit of publicity puts you more and more on the map.'

'Of course, my dear Count,' Skorzeny agreed slumping down into his armchair once more. 'My press,' he indicated the papers strewn all over the expensive Oriental carpet, 'has been good, very good indeed. Even that drunken sod Churchill said in the House of Commons yesterday that I had executed a brilliant abduction. Coming from an enemy that must be, I think, high praise indeed.'

Otto recalled abruptly the look on Student's face when he had flown in to Vienna twelve hours after they had finally landed there with a defective engine and five litres of gas left in the Storch's tanks. There had been angry talk of 'courts martial' and 'firing squads' until Skorzeny had wordlessly shown the crimson-faced, irate para General the personal cable of congratulations from Adolf Hitler himself. Student's mood had changed immediately; he had positively fawned over the man he had just been threatening to shoot. And it had been the same everywhere in Vienna over the last three days. The hotel suite had been flooded with expensive flowers and handwritten invitation cards from '*Herr Baron*' this and '*Herr Graf*' that. A good half a dozen times, Skorzeny's bodyguard had been forced to eject women who had somehow sneaked into his bedroom to 'offer myself to the hero'; and once a gushing middle-aged Viennese countess, who Otto soon found out was minus her underwear, made a very interesting and intricate sexual suggestion to the newly created SS Lieutenant in return for an introduction to the 'great man'. Being a hero, Otto had decided, had its compensations; the only problem was that being a hero meant that one had to continue executing heroic acts: an activity which meant that one got shot at, something which Otto personally regarded as unpleasant and decidedly dangerous.

The business of being a hero seemingly bothered Skorzeny, too, for suddenly a propos of nothing, he said, a note of almost pleading in his voice, 'Count, you are an experienced man. You have seen many places and done many strange things during your years with the *Abwehr*, serving our Führer in the mysterious way of the Secret Service,' he swallowed hard, his prominent Adam's apple running up and down his neck as if by lift, 'What . . . what can I do next?'

'Do next?' the Count echoed, putting down his white wine, momentarily puzzled, his 'SS voice' forgotten.

'Yes, I know just how fickle public opinion is. Look how Goebbels dropped Rommel after the defeat at El Alamein. Who talks of the Desert Fox these days? My press is good today, but how long will it last, how long?' He pulled his lace handkerchief from his sleeve and dabbed his nose.

Otto looked at him aghast and then at the Count, whose face revealed just how excited he was by the sudden challenge. He said a fervent prayer to heaven that for once, just once, the Count's quick wits would desert him.

But God was not listening to Otto Stahl that particular warm September afternoon in the year of 1943.

'Abduction,' he said.

For one gloriously happy moment Otto thought the

Count had said 'seduction' and he was just telling himself that the silly old fart had had the first sensible idea he had heard him express in all their years together, when Skorzeny repeated the word.

'*Abduction*?'

'Yes,' the Count said excitedly. 'Look how your abduction of the Duce has changed the whole situation in Northern Italy. A month ago it looked as if the *Wehrmacht* would have to evacuate the whole country and the Allies would have been at the Brenner within weeks. Now, thanks to Mussolini, we've got the country firmly under our control and soon there will be a new Italian republic established in the north.'

Skorzeny nodded his agreement and said, 'Carry on, my dear Count. Explain your plans.'

'They are these,' the Count barked in his new positive 'SS voice'. 'Systematic kidnapping of key figures on the enemy side. Why waste time, money and naturally good German blood, knocking out Soviet armies when the simple abduction of – Marshal Zhukov for instance – would cripple the Red Army's offensive spirit for months? Take out de Gaulle and the French resistance movement collapses, as if it had never existed. The French are really only interested in sex and food anyway.'

'*Great God in Heaven!*' Skorzeny breathed in awe, his dark eyes flashing excitedly, 'what a grandiose, brilliant idea, my friend! A totally new way of waging war, carried out by a handful of picked specialists such as ourselves.' He shot the Count and Otto a quick confident glance, 'specialists who go for the head instead of the fat guts or the flat feet! One man . . . one man alone abducted . . . and the whole enemy structure collapses like a house of cards. It's magnificent, Count! The Führer will love it!'

'*Stalin!*' the Count cried, face flushed crimson, as if he were very drunk.

'*Churchill!*' Skorzeny exclaimed exuberantly, not to be outdone.

'*Why not*?' the Count shrieked, springing to his feet, carried away completely by the mad excitement of the new idea. '*AMERICA*,' he screamed fervently, spittle flying everywhere, '*AND . . . AND*,' frantically he twisted his head to one side, gasping for breath, as if he were being strangled, '*AND . . . FRANKLIN DELANO . . . ROOSEVELT!*'

Otto could stand no more. His face contorted crazily, eyes refusing to see the two mad men dancing up and down in front of him, he clapped his hands tightly to his ears, trying to drown out the names. It was beginning all over again. *WOULD IT NEVER HAVE AN END?*